BEST

Lesbian

LOVE
STORIES

New York City

BEST

Lesbian

LOVE
STORIES

New
York
City

edited by

SIMONE THORNE

alyson books
NEW YORK

Manufactured in the United States of America.

This trade paperback original is published by
Alyson Books
P.O. Box 1253
Old Chelsea Station
New York, New York 10113-1251

Distribution in the United Kingdom by
Turnaround Publisher Services Ltd.
Unit 3, Olympia Trading Estate,
Coburg Road, Wood Green
London N22 6TZ England

First Edition: November 2006

06 07 08 09 00 a 10 9 8 7 6 5 4 3 2 1

ISBN 1-55583-972-X
ISBN-13 978-1-55583-972-7

Library of Congress Cataloging-in-Publication Data is on file.

CONTENTS

INTRODUCTION

LOVE HAS A way of finding you. I'd just graduated from university in Paris, but I was still longing to fully discover myself. It took the city of New York, to which I had just returned, and a beautiful woman, who showed me first love, to truly discover myself.

There we were, walking hand-in-hand down Manhattan's streets, kissing atop her Brooklyn apartment in full view of Lady Liberty, picnicking in Central Park, and dancing in the bars along the Hudson; love had crept its way into my heart. Ultimately we parted, but my love for New York only deepened.

Apparently, I'm not alone, as the stories in this year's collection of *Best Lesbian Love Stories* can attest. Whether it's celebrating an eternal love that leads us into the sunset or exploring the heart-breaking risks that love requires, there's something for everyone. Marilyn Jaye Lewis reveals hard lessons about how little we know about love in "Hard Girls Break Easy," and Diana Cage addresses infidelities in a "Momentary

Lapse of Reason." In "Hand's Free," Rachel Kramer Bussel explores sex as the ultimate way to express our feelings, while Katia Noyes exposes the alienation that many of us feel when we search for a connection, in "Prelude."

All in all, sixteen writers—each with her own unique spin—open their hearts to us with their words, their energy, and their passion. Here are stories for women who love women, for women who can't help but fall for a city that helped shape their lives.

To love!
Simone Thorne

THE POPULATION OF NEW YORK

AMIE EVANS

"SO, WHAT DID you think of my friend Kate?" Leah asks as she plops down on the sales counter next to my *Norton Anthology of American Literature.*

"Kate?" I ask, unsure of who exactly Kate is and why Leah would care what I thought of her.

"My friend, I just went to lunch with her. You met her an hour ago," Leah says, getting off the counter and grabbing a stack of hangers to put the new shirts on before we price them.

"Kate," I say, closing my anthology and grabbing a pile of the shirts to help her. "Cute. Not really your type."

"She thinks you are hot," Leah says giggling like a twelve-year-old schoolgirl.

"She's not really *my* type either," I say, placing a shirt

on the hanger then handing it to her to hang on the rack.

"She's a lit major at your school." I raise an eyebrow at this fact. "She's smart, cute, single. What's not your type about that?"

I tilt my head to the left. "I like my girlfriends a bit butchier or punkier, less standard-issue lesbian than Kate looks."

"Come on. She's very cool. She's a really good friend," Leah says, handing me the last shirt as she grabs the pricing gun. "Besides, the punkier, butchier set has really fucked you over lately." Leah, who is a ball of unlabeled lesbian sexual energy morphing from hot femme to hard-core butch in hours, had listened over the last six months as the three women I had dated each went from fab to freak. Cheating, dropping out, and reappearing, drama after drama, all of which I hate. I run my hand through my crew cut, then smooth my vintage dress with both hands.

"All right. If *she'll* ask me out, I'll say yes to one date with her."

Leah jumps up and down clapping her hands like a small child. I like Leah for her ability to behave childishly at the drop of a hat. Her joy over small things inspires me. I wish I could be less serious and more spontaneous like her. "A date—that's all I will agree to. I cannot make any promises to anything more than one date."

"No. One date is perfect. Really, she's been watching you for weeks."

"What? You have to tell me. Did I just agree to go out with a stalker?"

As it turned out Kate rides the same bus as I do from school to St. Mark's Place every day. She'd noticed me weeks ago and had attempted repeatedly to catch my eye. My head is continuously buried in homework on the bus since I am terminally overextended between school, an on-campus work study position, and this part-time job at the funky clothing store Trash and Vaudeville. I'd never even seen this dyke checking me out. Had I noticed her, I wasn't sure I'd have flirted back. She was, after all, an issue-cut campus dyke with jeans, button-down shirts, and radical feminist pins on her backpack. Not my normal dating selection, but as Leah had pointed out my taste in women hadn't been panning out so well for me lately. But still, was I that out of touch that I didn't even see a dyke flirting with me? Perhaps Kate was just what I needed—the exact opposite of what I would normally consider datable—to add some nondrama fun back into my life. And maybe a little casual sex would clear my mind and reset my karma.

Two days later, I'm at the coffee shop on my break reading Milton's *Paradise Lost*, contemplating serving in heaven versus ruling in hell. Deciding I am currently serving in hell, Kate walks in. She's wearing jeans and a blue ski jacket. She's holding her backpack in one hand with a purple pin announcing *i love women* and a white pin declaring *if you don't believe in abortion, don't have one.* I wonder why I agreed to do this. Kate has short brown hair and a slender body with a thin face. She is attractive even though she is issue cut. And there is a hint of butch in her walk and how she holds her body.

She scans the room until she sees me, then smiles and walks over to my table. I smile back and gesture for her to sit down. I place my still open book face down on the table as she sits. I want to get this over with so I can finish my homework before my break ends and go straight to bed after I close the store at 11:00 p.m. I'm already exhausted.

"So," I say, taking a sip of coffee and putting the cup back on the table. "Leah said you had something to ask me."

"Yeah," Kate says, looking at me. I notice her eyes are brown, full of warmth and a bit of playfulness. Then she looks at the table top and back to me before quickly returning her gaze to the table. She suddenly looks awkward and nervous.

I'm instantly annoyed. All she has to do is ask; she knows I'll say yes. Leah told her I would. I like take-charge butches and she appears to be neither butch nor take-charge. I want to finish reading the next ten pages before returning to work. I'm only doing this as a favor to Leah and my patience is small and frail. I'm not interested in this date.

"Well, what is it?" I say sounding cockier and colder than I had intended.

"What's the population of New York?" Kate asks deadpan, then smiles. Her smile's light and playful, but it's apparent from the shake in her voice that she really is nervous.

Caught completely off guard by her question, I laugh. I pick up my book and bend the page I was reading then place it closed on the table. I lean forward, closer to her, and in a low voice say, "Well, Kate"— I use her name to see how it feels in my mouth then pause and slide back in my seat a bit, forcing her to lean in closer to hear me—"I don't know the answer to that question." I lean the rest of the way back into my chair and pick up my coffee and take the last sip before setting it back down. I let the silence fill the air between us and watch her face as she processes my answer and ponders quickly what to say next. I feel as cocky as I sound, so before she can speak I add, "But, I'll tell you what. How about if I look it up and we meet for dinner on Wednesday? I'll let you know what the population of New York is then."

"Wednesday would be great," she says, a flush of pink rising in her face. She stands up and starts to leave. "See you Wednesday at six?"

"Seven. Meet me at Trash. I get off at seven." I wink.

"Seven. Wednesday." Kate winks back and is gone out the door before I see the blue ski gloves on the table. I tuck them along with my book into my bag. I giggle as I get up and leave.

I feel light and airy. I feel good and suddenly I'm interested in Kate. I'm refreshed by her innocence or lack of attitude; I haven't exactly figured out which it is. Her bashfulness, real or an act, was a relief and so different from the women I am normally drawn to. I quiz Leah about her when I return to work. Kate is cochair of the feminist group on campus. She's a women's studies minor. I'm tantalized by her, fascinated by what she could possibly find of interest in me, a postmodern punk femme.

At school, I look up the population of New York on the Internet. I feel a bit giddy, school girlish. Meeting for dinner under the pretense that I will provide her with a bit of information she most likely doesn't care about and most certainly could find in two minutes herself if she did want it: It reminds me of an intricate plot of a Victorian novel or a junior high school plan to get kisses from boys.

On Wednesday night, Kate meets me at work and we walk two blocks to a Chinese restaurant we have both been to before. She is wearing jeans and a light blue button-down shirt under her ski jacket. I've got on a beige vintage cotton day dress with tiny red flowers, and combat boots. Again I wonder why I am here and think how odd we must look together.

At the restaurant we look over the menus, settling into a familiar rhythm of a date, calming ourselves, setting our expectations or releasing them. We are surrounded by cheap Chinese art and plastic sculptures, but we both know this place has the best food in all NYC outside of Chinatown.

"Do you want to order two dishes and share?" Kate asks.

I am immediately reminded of my childhood and say, "Yes." Then I wonder as I look over the menu what dish she'll pick.

"I like General Tsao's." She smiles at me over the top of her menu. "Do you?"

"I've never had it, but I'll give it a try." I giggle, thinking that could be the theme of this evening. "I like shrimp egg foo yung. Do you?" I say mimicking her question.

"Perfect." After ordering, Kate pours both of us tea then leans forward toward me, resting her elbows on the table and folding her hands, and says, "Tell me a story."

I look at her blankly. "A story?" I ask, confused.

"Yes. Tell me a story about you, something from your life, your past." My mind goes completely blank. A story about my past? I don't seem to have had a past at this moment as I search my brain for one single thing of interest to tell her. I look at her. She smiles. Her eyes are warm and intent. She is waiting and interested. "Anything?" I ask.

"Anything at all," she says.

I tell her about growing up in a small town in New Jersey. I tell her about the ocean and the sand and the seagulls. I tell her about my childhood cat, Midnight. I tell her about my hippy parents who do art for a living. I tell her about my prim and proper grandmother. I tell her about learning to drive and going to Catholic school. And she laughs and asks questions about details and makes connections between the stories I tell her.

Kate tells me about growing up in Pittsburgh, Pennsylvania, and about her childhood cat, Patches, and her sisters. She tells me about how her great-grandmother, grandmother, and grandaunt all purchased a house in 1925 and raised Kate's mother alone together in it after her grandfather had left. She speaks with reverence about what strong women they were. She tells me about how her mother died when she was only sixteen. And before I realize it, dinner is over and the evening is gone and it is late and time to go home.

Kate pays for dinner, insisting I can buy next time. And we leave the restaurant as a light snow starts to fall. "Oh," I say, opening my backpack and pulling out her gloves, "you left these at the coffee shop." I hand them to her.

She puts them into her pocket. "Thanks. I thought I lost them for good." And then she calmly takes my hand. "Can I walk you home?"

"Yes."

We walk back toward my apartment, holding hands. The snow collects on the street signs and parked cars, and on our shoulders and heads. I feel warm and comfortable. We talk about Russian literature and American versus French feminism. Kate tells me she works at the Museum of Natural Science to pay for school. She offers to show it to me and tells me we can get in for free.

We stop at my building, just a few blocks from St. Mark's Place. "This is it," I say. She looks at the stone archway and the large metal security door. I point to the button for apartment number five. "That's me; I live alone," I say, then immediately feel stupid.

She pushes the buzzer and we laugh, then silence fills the air.

"18,976,457," I say and Kate looks at me, confused. "The population of New York. I told you I'd look it up." Kate smiles, blushes, and looks down at her feet. "It is why we had dinner, after all," I say, teasingly brushing some snow off her shoulder.

"Yes, it is," she says, nodding her head, then reaches into her backpack and pulls a small note pad and pen out. "Write it down for me."

I take the pad and write the words "Population of New York" followed by the number, then "Amanda" and my phone number. I hand it back to her. She looks at it and smiles, then leans against the stone archway and takes my hand.

Our faces inches from each other and our hands entwined, she says, "I'll call you."

"Yes, please do," I say. Then I lean against the cold stone archway and pull her by the hand in closer to me. "Call me," I whisper then press my lips against hers. She kisses me back and we both open our lips and allow our tongues in to explore our mouths. I feel instantly warm and tingly. Her kiss is perfect, not too hard or soft, not too wet or dry. And then we part, separate from each other. We both laugh.

"Bye," she says, walking down the street.

I stand in the doorway, watching her walk to the end of the block and turn the corner, before letting myself into the entry way.

. . . . .

ON THURSDAY, I look for Kate on the bus but don't see her. When I get home I have two voicemail messages. The first is from Kate who leaves her number, which I write on the pad next to the phone. Her voice is musical and I save the message. The second is from Andrea. The sound of her voice on my machine takes my breath away. Andrea whom I've been lusting after for six months. Andrea who is elusive and untouchable. Andrea who is a walking duplicate of my sexual fantasy. Andrea, punky, butch with a purple Mohawk and a tattoo on the curve of her right arm, is calling me for a date.

I call Andrea back immediately and we set up a dinner date for Wednesday. My heart is pounding and my mind is racing when I get off the phone. I make tea and settle down to do my reading. I'm surprised when all I can think about is Kate.

I wait two whole days, a full forty-eight hours before returning Kate's call. I'm a bit freaked out by my inability to get her out of my mind. When I call, she sounds excited. I remain composed, together, unmoved. I tell her I had fun. I tell her I'd like to see her again. She tells me she has to work on Wednesday. I tell her I have a date on Wednesday anyway. I listen as her tone goes from giddy to distant. I tell her Thursday would work. She agrees tentatively. We chat about going to a movie or to the museum where she works. She tells me she doesn't normally date more than one person and thought our date went well. I tell her I do date more than one person. She says she is interested in me and thought I was into her. I don't answer. I say we can talk on Thursday. We say goodnight and hang up.

I feel bad, despite the fact that I haven't done anything wrong. I spend the next few days telling myself I haven't done anything wrong. We are just dating and I have a right to date other people. I tell myself I have a responsibility to tell Kate I have a date with someone else. I spend those days leading up to my first date with Andrea—hot, sexy, butch Andrea—thinking about Kate.

There was something cute and innocent about Kate's shyness. But that wasn't enough to keep me fixated on her. There was something concrete and real about her. She wanted to know about me—about who I was. Not just who I wanted her to think I was, but more importantly, who I actually was. What my life experiences were and how they'd shaped who I had become. Kate was so unlike anyone I had ever dated before. She'd gotten under my skin.

. . . . .

WEDNESDAY NIGHT I meet Andrea at the same Chinese restaurant Kate and I went to for our first date. Andrea has on vinyl pants and a mesh shirt over a camouflage bra. I am wearing a black vintage dress with tiny rhinestones set into the plunging neckline, and combat boots. I think we look charming together.

I suggest we order two dishes and share them. Andrea says she'd rather not. After ordering, Andrea talks about local dyke punk bands and the clubs she likes to dance at. Andrea is a business major, but her real passion is music. I try to imagine her at Morgan Stanley or Ernst & Young but cannot. She talks about how hard school is and how much fun she is having in NYC. She doesn't work; her parents are paying for everything. I tell her she is lucky. She tells me her parents don't understand her. They are demanding. Andrea tells me how much she wants to get another tattoo and that she is thinking of getting her nipples pierced, but she thinks it will hurt too much. I have mine pierced and start to tell her about it but she cuts me off and tells me about how a good friend of hers is friends with a woman who is best friends with the lead singer of Tribe8 and how she got to party with Tribe8. She offers to arrange for me to party with them. Andrea begins to tell me about why punk is important to the dyke movement. Andrea doesn't ask me one question about myself.

"I just realized something," I say, getting up and

putting my coat on. "I have to go."

"What? Dinner hasn't come yet."

"I know, I am sorry. Let me leave some money," I say pulling ten dollars from my wallet.

Andrea doesn't say anything. I place the money on the table, smile, and leave. As soon as I am out of the restaurant, I run. I run as fast as I can down the street to the train station and down the steps to the platform.

The subway ride to the museum takes forever. I rehearse over and over in my head what I will say to Kate. When I finally arrive I go around back to the service entry and ask the guard at the door to page Kate. I smile uncomfortably at him and tell him I'm her sister and there is an emergency. He calls Kate on her walkie-talkie and tells me I can wait in the hall.

Everything—the floor, ceiling, and walls—in the hall is painted the same shade of light gray. Most likely it has an enchanting name like Gun Bolt Gray or Steel Gray but really it is a dense toneless gray that can be found in every institutional setting in every city in the United States. I sit in the chair by the door with my hands folded in my lap, my heart beating, and my mind racing. I feel very much like I am waiting to be called by the grade school principal for something I have been caught doing and will soon be punished for.

Kate arrives via a door at the end of the hall. She walks toward me and I stand up. She is wearing black uniform pants with a white button-down security shirt with the museum's logo and security shields on the arm. She has a black tie around her neck and a number of items attached to her belt. She looks really butch and my heart skips a beat.

"Hi," I say, not sure how to start.

"Hi," she says looking me over. "Come with me." She leads me down the hallway to another door which she unlocks with a master key. We go up two flights of steps and into another short hallway that spills out onto one of the galleries of natural history. The walls are lined with exhibits depicting primeval earth's plants and animals and early cavemen hunting. In the middle of the room, the massive bones of a T. rex are assembled. Kate walks over and leans against the railing protecting the dinosaur from visitors. I stand next to her, looking up at the imposing frame of the T. rex. "There are no cameras in this exhibit hall so we can talk privately," she says.

I look at her and nod. "I—" I actually don't know what to say, despite my rehearsal. I feel confused and flooded with emotion. Nothing is as it should be. I just left Andrea at the restaurant and I am not sure why I ran here. My world is all mixed up.

"I thought you had a date tonight," Kate says, looking at her watch.

"I did." I smile. Take a deep breath. "It was terrible. I mean, it was fine, but the whole time I was sitting there with her"—I look down at the fake plants at T. rex's feet—"all I could think of was, well, you."

I look up at her. She smiles. "Really?" And that

warmth and playfulness come back into her eyes.

"Yes, silly, do you think I'd take the train over here and say I was your sister if it wasn't true?"

"So, what does that mean?"

"I guess it means that I'm interested in you."

"You guess."

"I'm interested in you."

Kate grabs my hand and pulls me into her, wrapping one arm around my waist and cupping the other behind my neck. "I'm interested in you, too," she says, then leans in and kisses me hard. "And, there aren't any cameras in this exhibit."

"Really," I say.

"Really," she repeats, then pressing her body hard against mine, our lips meet, and I close my eyes.

HARD GIRLS BREAK EASY

MARILYN JAYE LEWIS

MAY I DRAW your attention to the simple neighborhood of Woodside in the borough of Queens, New York, and to the not very attractive part of it, to boot? It was there, in a modest apartment in one of countless towering high-rises, that there once lived a very beautiful girl named Pearl. She was a grown woman by the time we met in Manhattan but she'd grown up there in Woodside, in that ugly dot on the urban map. Pearl had been the proverbial gem in a five-and-dime store; meaning, on the teeming streets of Queens, in its seventy *thousand* acres of overly developed, mostly concrete land, what was one more dark-haired, brown-eyed Jewish girl among its millions of inhabitants? And what could be said about the state of her shimmering soul?

Nothing. For that, you needed to zoom in much closer. A bed would do. But two girls up close in a bed came later, almost by accident. And two girls *in love* in a bed came a couple years after that.

I'd always lived in Manhattan, from the moment I'd stepped foot in New York. For me, Manhattan *was* New York and the boroughs were nothing but a vast wilderness. Okay, a densely populated vast wilderness with too many cars and a lot of noisy, hopelessly congested expressways. But a wilderness nonetheless—of the intellect. Perhaps I thought the boroughs were too reminiscent of where I'd come from, a suburbia that sprawled out to infinity while deftly camouflaging any cultural advantages it might have been harboring. Nowadays, you hear about all sorts of trendy "culture" exploding in New York's boroughs, but this is a relatively recent development in the history of highbrow New York City–style culture. A development brought on by the twin sirens of necessity and greed.

In an earlier less-expensive era, not so long ago it seems, the world itself revolved around Manhattan. The city never felt like the island it was, it felt more like the sun. Day or night, it had its own peculiar heat that everyone flew toward and thrived on. The city was dirtier then—more litter, more pollution, more petty crimes. Still, it remained what it had always been, an eternally romantic backdrop for love when you were lucky enough to find it.

When I first met Pearl, the only thing we had in

common was that we were both brown-eyed brunettes and we were both hoping to be famous. We both sang and played guitars in our own bands. There the similarities ended. She was into punk rock. I was into folk music. I was a musical puritan, of sorts. She was a radical, an innovator. She'd grown up hard in the city, while I hadn't turned hard until I'd come to New York and had made the less glamorous side of it my home.

One of my contemporaries back then, my rival on the folk music scene, a wisp of a blonde named Millie Duvall, did become famous. Very famous, in fact. And Millie had gone to the same high school as Pearl. In school, Millie, who was totally hetero, had rarely given Pearl anything but the time of day. Still Pearl had been smitten with Millie as only lesbian teenage girls can be smitten with straight girls—in the hard, agonizing, all-consuming way. The crush on Millie was a still-tender history by the time I met Pearl. The two of them were passively civilized to each other on the music scene, and it was because of Millie that my path had crossed Pearl's at all.

I opened for Millie Duvall one Saturday night at a popular folk club on MacDougal Street. I met Pearl that same night in the club's pathetic excuse for a dressing room, between sets. She was wearing black jeans, black Converse high-tops, and a black motorcycle jacket. Her brown hair hung in gentle waves to her shoulders, and she kept it scooped behind each ear, revealing single gold rings in each pierced lobe. She was tall and thin as a rail and wore no makeup at all; she was naturally beautiful.

I had my own crew in tow in that tiny dressing room, so I can't honestly say I noticed her before she quietly asked if she could use my lighter. In those days, we both smoked. And as it later turned out, it wasn't our worst vice. I was too preoccupied with my envy over Millie's rising fame to make any small talk with her entourage beyond, "sure," when Pearl asked to borrow the lighter. It was Pearl who started the conversation.

"That was a good set," she said.

"Really?" I was genuinely surprised by the compliment. Most people hanging out in a dressing room between sets did not usually see the opening acts.

She smiled ironically. "Yeah, really. I enjoyed it. Why? Didn't you think you were good?"

To be honest, I'd thought I'd been very good and I thought the audience had thought so, too, which had only served to heighten my envy of Millie Duvall—a singer I considered average at best, and a songwriter I considered mediocre. Yet she was the one with the record deal and I was the one warming up her audience. "I'm happy with it," I said. "It felt pretty good on my end."

"Well, it was good." Pearl lit her cigarette and handed the lighter back to me: a gesture so ordinary as to be unnoticeable and yet within a few short weeks it would become a gesture infused with intimacy as we lit our cigarettes in bed after making love; a gesture that would underlie the growing familiarity between us. She never managed to hold onto a lighter for very long or to have so much as a book of matches on her person for any length of time, least of all in a bed other than her own.

"Do you perform here a lot?" Pearl went on, standing closer to me. Not that it meant anything; the tiny dressing room was crowded.

"I play all up and down this block and in the clubs over on Bleecker and West Third Streets."

"All of Millie's haunts, huh?"

"I guess you could say that, but I'd be playing them whether or not Millie Duvall existed."

Apparently, bitterness uncoils its tongue independent of the speaker. I certainly hadn't intended to sound so petulant, least of all to someone who was obviously in the Millie Duvall camp.

Pearl smiled broadly over that comment. "She is a bit of a musical dilettante, isn't she? But she's a hardworking one."

That threw me. It made me wonder what my own crew might be saying about me when I was out of earshot. "That's kind of a strange remark," I said.

"But it's an honest one. Millie and I go way back. We both studied music at the High School of Performing Arts. I know what she does and doesn't know about music."

"So you're a musician, too, then?"

"Yeah."

"Do you play out much?" Talk about dilettante, I

thought. In that motorcycle jacket, she could only be some kind of rock and roller.

"Yeah. I have an all-girl band called the Nasty Fucks."

It was finally my turn to smile. "Are you serious?"

"Yeah, I'm serious."

"Do the clubs actually give you billing out front with a name like that?"

"Once in a while—the ones farther downtown that are only open after midnight do. And they don't book any fucking folk singers, I can tell you that much. Hey, you know, you're even prettier when you smile?"

It was a comment that caught me off guard—it implied that I was pretty regardless, just *prettier* when I smiled—and it flattered my considerable ego.

I soon learned that Pearl wasn't like most of the punk rockers that haunted the clubs around the Bowery. She was open to all kinds of music. And she could read and write music, even though all she ever played on her electric guitar was chords. It was all I ever played, too, only my guitar was acoustic. So we had that other thing in common. In spite of our brown hair, our brown eyes, our slender frames, and pretty faces, we responded to rhythm, to the savage muse. It pulsed in our blood. A devotion to fancy melodies was for a fussier type of musician, like Millie Duvall, who got radio airplay. We thrived instead on a straight-ahead rhythm accompanied by words. I favored stories that tore at the heart; Pearl favored staccato outbursts of rage. Still it all came down to rhythm and words.

There was a rhythm to the subway trains back then, a rhythm to the traffic in the noisy late-night streets. Our bodies fell into the rhythm from that first moment we left the folk club together on MacDougal Street, missing Millie's act and choosing to go someplace noisier for a beer instead. "I thought Millie was a friend of yours," I fished curiously. "Why didn't you want to stay and listen to her set?"

"Well, for one thing, I've heard her a million times before and, frankly, 'friend' is putting a sanitized label on what she is to me."

We fell into the rhythm of confessions almost immediately and it set the tempo for the rest of our tumultuous affair. "What does *that* mean?"

Pearl focused momentarily on her mug of beer, then said rather poetically, "Millie taught me the meaning of words like 'beloved' and 'cherish' and 'anguish' and 'ache.' Words that get into your veins and cut you to ribbons, especially when the cherished beloved does nothing but ignore you and send your world spiraling into constant heartbreak. Have you ever loved a girl in that way? A straight girl who didn't have a clue? I had her on a pedestal for four long years that felt like a lifetime. I worshipped her from afar and watched her leave school everyday in the car of some older guy who wasn't in school anymore and who wasn't any good for her, in my smitten opinion. Not that my opinion would have meant shit to Millie Duvall."

I knew she was serious and yet I laughed. I couldn't help myself. It was so bitter and pathetic and melodramatic all in one. "Wow," I said, never dreaming that it would soon rather aptly describe how I would fall for Pearl. "You're right, I guess 'friend' doesn't come close. I'm kind of amazed that you're even *friendly* after a history like that."

She laughed then, too. "Oh, she's all right. I fell in love with a figment of my imagination. It had nothing to do with Millie, with who she really was, you know? I see it now." Then she added, "Did you ever fall in love with a straight girl?"

"Of course. But then I was always too enamored of myself to get that carried away with someone who wasn't into me."

"Well, aren't you a smart cookie."

And I did think I was smart. I thought I knew everything, especially how to stay one step ahead of the ball and chain of love. I could fall into bed with any girl but my heart kept a safe distance. Until Pearl, I was more interested in the spectacle of lust. Romance was okay for an evening as long as it led to sex. Otherwise, I kept it "just friends" and I concentrated on my career.

Not that I fell in love with Pearl right away, but when I fell, I fell hard. And unexpectedly. I'd had a dream one night that Pearl and I were in bed, making love with all our clothes on, and in the dream I felt like I'd known her forever, that she'd been important to me in a previous life and I was only now connecting her to the Pearl I knew in this life. The dream was fraught with meaning, a meaning that regrettably did not carry over into the waking world. All that lingered was a feeling of deep loss and it haunted me.

"Who *were* we?" I blurted one night while we were lying on my bed. We weren't making love yet. We were mostly still dressed, smoking cigarettes and each nursing a bottle of beer in the dark. The LCD of the stereo monitor was the only light in the room.

"What do you mean?" she said, cocking her head to one side and studying me intently.

At that moment, I fell into her brown eyes. I couldn't help myself. They seemed luminous in that electronic glow. In some inexplicable way, that look she had on her face triggered the memory of my dream in spades. "Do you think we could have known each other in another life?" I asked.

"I don't know. I suppose so."

"Isn't it weird that we would meet up again, then, in this one?"

"Maybe we agreed to meet again," she offered thoughtfully.

I was surprised she was taking me seriously, let alone taking it to the next level. I'd had no idea she was at all metaphysical. Like so many other downtown musicians, Pearl had veered from the beer and smokes and the occasional recreational drug use, onto the heroin route. I didn't think she had a problem with it (after all, she wasn't an addict, was she?), still I thought that even dabbling in hard narcotics automatically made her less spiritual. So her response surprised me.

"You never know," she continued, her gaze not flinching from mine in that soothing glow of the stereo receiver. "Who's to say that in some other life, we weren't talking together just like this, about knowing each other in a past life and then we agreed to meet again in this one. Shall we go ahead and agree to meet in the next one, as well?"

The sex between us that night felt more like making love than any sex had ever felt to me before. I felt connected to her from some other realm and I'd never made love to anyone that I'd ever paused long enough to feel connected to. After that night, I was hooked. I was the addict. I became obsessed with Pearl.

Not long afterward, her band went on a tour of Europe and she was gone for nearly a year. In her absence, I wrote a slew of thick, saccharine-y love songs that no one on the folk music circuit could stand to hear me sing, and I started drinking heavily—the hard stuff, like bourbon, straight up, a fifth of it every other night—and no other woman who came into my field of vision interested me in the slightest. I missed Pearl. I ached for her. I agonized over my searing desire to make love to her again. To be intimate with her. I cherished her. She was my beloved.

I knew then what it was like to have words seep into your veins and cut you to ribbons from the inside.

I was drying out from the booze when Pearl came

back from Europe. In a surprising move, she moved back in with her newly widowed mom in Woodside. Pearl called unexpectedly in the middle of the night. "I'm home," she said, her voice sounding worn out. "You want to come visit?"

Did I? The following day, I couldn't get out to Queens fast enough. It took me nearly two hours and three different trains to get there from the Lower East Side.

When I came up from out of the subway, it seemed incongruous to me, that my cherished beloved was back there in ugly Woodside, in that nondescript apartment with her grieving mother, in that room where she'd grown up. Standing in it, I felt awed, like I was in some sacred place. But all it was was a room; four cheap walls and a ceiling that had sheltered an overly sensitive Jewish girl from her tortuous crush on Millie Duvall. Oh, she of the wispy blonde hair and strictly hetero lifestyle.

Then I came to learn that the little bedroom in Woodside was a haven against Pearl's heroin habit. She'd been hospitalized in Europe to try to kick it. For now, her veins were clean and she was taking it one day at a time, like everybody else I knew.

It was a temperament that matched mine perfectly. "You want to sit down?" she said, indicating her single bed where, on some metaphysical plane, her girlhood nights of anguish still lingered. I was certain of it.

"Okay," I said. I perched on the edge of it tentatively. She had become larger than life to me. It was hard to sit so close to her and not feel overwhelmed by my own needs.

"I love you, Pearl," I blurted.

"I love you, too," she said. But it came easily to her, the words sounded too matter-of-fact, like barely a thought had gone into the saying of them.

I held it against her, the ease with which she could say, "I love you." And even though we spent some quality quiet time together, doing healthy things and being healthy girls out in the bright sunshine—or as bright as it gets in Manhattan—I wanted to hear the kind of "I love you" words that were cutting her to ribbons inside.

The sex was good. Sober sex is always a rush after having chemically-induced dead sex for a time, but it was clear that Pearl was in complete control of whatever passion she was harboring for me. It was not the all-consuming love, as mine was; it wasn't the same love, the love I eventually insisted it had to be if we were ever going to share it.

In hindsight, there were too many things we each needed to learn about life to not have ended our big romance. Pearl is a healthy woman now. So healthy, in fact, that she owns her own health food store up in Woodstock and has been with the same equally healthy woman for sixteen years. How do I know this? Because I'm still playing folk music on the folk circuit. I never made enough money to retire, as Millie Duvall did so many years ago. I play all the small clubs up and down the Eastern Seaboard, and all along the Hudson River. I was in a pathetic excuse for a dressing room upstate one night, still the opening act, when Pearl dropped in from out of nowhere to say hello. Still no makeup and still as naturally beautiful as ever. I was surprised she had sought me out, of her own volition, no less; surprised that the sight of me tuning up my guitar made her smile.

"Hey there, stranger," she said.

"Pearl! Gosh, you look good." I was quietly astounded by her sudden shining presence in my cranky, grown-up world.

Later, after my set, we spent a few more minutes chatting before she had to head back home. And I noticed that her eyes crinkled pleasingly when she smiled. It was age creeping up on her and it suited her. I said, "You look happy, you know that?"

"I am happy," she said. "And how about you? Happy, too?"

Overwhelmed by a surprising flare-up of an ancient aching need, I croaked out, "Happy enough." And it wasn't a lie, per se. I *was* happy enough—for someone who finds herself suddenly buried alive in regret. That woman had once been in my bed, that gem in a five-and-dime store, Pearl; the most beautiful woman in the world. She'd readily said she loved me and I hadn't believed that love could be real if it didn't hurt.

I followed her out to her car. "I'm sorry," I said pathetically.

"Sorry for what?"

"For not letting love be enough, I guess."

She seemed to understand what I was referring to and it made my heart ache even more. I had been so clumsy about loving her, so self-involved. I'd have given anything at that moment to take it all back and rewrite it, start over. "It's okay," she said. "If it makes you feel any better, I loved you a whole lot more after you were gone, when I couldn't do anything about it. Weird, huh?"

What could I say? It did make me feel less like a loser. To be loved at all, even in hindsight, is a precious thing. I was grateful for it.

I watched her drive away until her taillights disappeared over a hill in the darkness. And I made a mental note to learn from this feeling, really learn from it, so that I wouldn't make the same mistake when I crossed her path in the next life, the next time her love came back around.

A MOMENTARY LAPSE OF REASON

DIANA CAGE

THE LAST TIME I saw her, though I didn't know it would be the last, she rolled up my street in a beat-up Dodge sedan she'd borrowed from her folks in Jersey. I was overly conscious of my hair and makeup and clothes that afternoon and I remember distinctly the pencil skirt, clingy T-shirt with the neck cut out, and stiletto mules I'd chosen for the occasion. I'd straightened my hair, applied liquid eyeliner and copious amounts of perfume. It'd been more than two years since we'd seen each other in person and I worried she'd no longer find me attractive. I always did that. I always worried that I wouldn't be found attractive by my lovers. It never occurred to me that I might be the one to lose interest, to move on, until it happened.

I was standing in front of my apartment in Bushwick

that I shared with my girlfriend and two dogs. It was hot—midsummer hot. There were kids playing in the street and the ice-cream truck jangle played incessantly over and over and over. The lady next door screamed angrily at the driver in Spanish to turn it off but I only caught half of what she said.

I stood frozen and anxious, hip cocked to one side, posing as provocatively as I could manage. She parked quickly and stared at me for a beat before getting out of the car. She looked all wrong: hair too short, wrinkled khakis, faded black T-shirt, sweaty and red-faced from the hot drive. And I nearly changed my mind. I nearly said, *Go back home. I don't want you.* Then we were kissing. Her hands were in my hair, around my throat, holding my waist, and I was thinking, *So this is what it's like to cheat. It's not so bad really.*

When we finally disengaged, Janey said, "I've missed you." And I said, "Yeah, me too."

She hadn't brought much, just a gym bag with a change of pants, a short sleeve button-down shirt, some flip-flops, some cute boxers from the Gap, a pair of Ray-Bans, and a bunch of grooming products. I remarked on her small bag and she said, "I'm not moving in, I'm just around for the weekend, remember? How long is Cassy gone?"

"Till Thursday," I replied.

"What are we doing?" I said, racked again with guilt. Though it was an odd guilt. I didn't actually feel guilty about cheating. It was just in the abstract I knew I was doing something wrong. People aren't supposed to invite ex-lovers for the weekend when their girlfriend is out of town. I'd told Cassy an old friend from San Francisco was visiting. She said she was sorry she wouldn't get to meet her.

Janey's hands were different than Cassy's. I think I'd forgotten what she looked like. Her fingers were shorter and wider. And her palms were wider. Her forearms were thicker and more muscular than my girlfriend's, too. She was a stockier girl. Her muscles turned me on. That much I remember. That much was the same. I handed her a Budweiser from the fridge and watched her wrap her fingers around it. "Thank you baby," she said. Then I poured myself a very tall shot of Jim Beam and sat across from her on our cracked vinyl kitchen chairs. The kitchen was immaculate. I'd scrubbed the floors, cleaned the stove, and put everything in its place before her arrival. It was more out of neurotic energy than it was a desire for neatness.

. . . . .

THE FIRST TIME we met I lived in San Francisco. It was before Cassy, before moving across the country, before turning thirty and deciding I should settle into my life a little and stop being such a child. I was sitting at the bar near my house, an overpriced dive owned by a pair of lovely Irish dykes. The bartender poured with a heavy hand. I was hammered, having taken a

Clonopin and a shot of whiskey before I left the house in an attempt to stave off an anxiety attack. To my right sat my girlfriend's best friend. She'd just finished explaining that my girlfriend had been cheating on me with her ex since the inception of our relationship. "I can't believe she was porking that dimwitted cow," I slurred unkindly, and then began crying.

"Are you going to be OK?" she asked as she put a hand on my shoulder to steady me. But I was fine. I was just drunk. I wasn't even really upset. It was more like extreme annoyance. Like my relationship had been a very large mosquito and I'd finally been bitten. I hate this town, I thought. I hate all the queers here. I hate that I can't swing my handbag without knocking the glasses off some dyke. And then in walked someone I'd never seen before. She sat down next to us and introduced herself. She had a brownish shaggy mop, gray eyes, broad shoulders, and a sexy fucking grin. She was ballsy enough to look at my red-rimmed eyes and offer me a drink.

"I'm J," she said.

"J?" I slurred. "Like, J-A-Y? Or is it short for something?"

"It's short for Janey," she explained. "But I like J better."

"Oh. Well, hi J," I slurred. "Uh, I'm not normally so drunk you know. I mean, I just found out I was dating an unfaithful jerk. And she wasn't even very smart. Plus she was clingy. I don't even know how she had time to cheat on me. She was always so busy being clingy. And she sucked in bed, too." Then I pitched forward off my bar stool and Janey caught me.

I'd already made up my mind to move to New York. But I asked Janey to come home with me anyway. And we spent the next four days straight together. She bought a toothbrush and a contact lens case from the Walgreens on the corner and just stayed in my apartment. We didn't change clothes or go out.

For three and a half days we showered together, slept together, spent the afternoons reading and talking together. We did everything except have sex. No matter how many times I tried I couldn't let myself fuck her. I had that feeling I get when I'm going to fall in love. Like vertigo. I felt high and dizzy and unstable. And every time her fingers strayed near my crotch I stopped her.

"We can see each other when I come back from my trip," Janey kept telling me. But I knew we wouldn't. I knew I'd be gone and she'd be in California and I would pine for something impractical and painful. That's the thing about me: I have willpower when I need it. And a very well developed sense of self-protection. And I wasn't going to let go and get hurt by some shaggy girlboy with a cute grin and big gray eyes.

I got up every morning and made us coffee and toast and crawled back in bed and talked to her about moving to New York. She talked to me about Indonesia; she was about to leave on a six-week business trip and I knew we wouldn't see each other again. When she left we promised to send postcards. And we did.

We also spent hundreds of dollars in cell phone bills. Intercontinental phone sex is pricey. Her half she expensed. Her design firm didn't bat an eye. My half meant I had to take on a monotonous freelance project. I spent two weeks laying out a five-hundred-page business report for an organization that wanted to "increase office productivity" but really they wanted to change policy so that disability leave was harder to get.

. . . . .

CASS AND I had been together for two years. We were very happy. We met almost as soon as I was settled in Brooklyn. A friend from college had introduced us. I knew I liked her right away. It just seemed right. Like she was girlfriend material. And I was still crazy about her. It wasn't that I wanted to break up with her. It's just that Janey had left me curious. I hate not knowing things. I can't stand it. It itches. And Janey couldn't take it either. About six months after I left town I called her. Ostensibly, just to say hi. But really I was setting a plan in motion.

"We need some music," I said. I was so fucking nervous. I'd really only been in this woman's presence for that four-day period in San Francisco and suddenly I had her in my house, the one I shared with my partner of two years, for the whole freaking weekend. I put on a mixed CD Cassy had made for a trip we took together. It was a lot of Brit pop mixed together with a few random songs like Dolly Parton's "Jolene," some Metallica, old Country, stuff she knew I liked.

For our first anniversary Cassy and I took a trip to Bakersfield. Cassy has a thing for a certain brand of country music and a certain type of country kitsch. Buck Owens owns a steak house in Bakersfield and played two shows a night there. I read up on it before we went, learned all about the Bakersfield sound. It's where Buck Owens, Merle Haggard, and a bunch of other singers got started. I was already in love with her but that trip cemented it. We ate giant, hideous chicken fried steaks so big they hung over the plate. They were delicious in that way that fried things are delicious. After we finished a bottle of wine, Cassy swung me out onto the dance floor while Buck crooned to us. I felt so in love with her.

And yet here I was with Janey. She reached across the table and touched my hand.

"So," she said. "How about we get in bed?"

I gulped my Jim Beam and said, "I can't fall in love with you."

"I'm not worried about that right now," she said. And then she grabbed me and pulled me down onto my well-scrubbed kitchen floor. I tried not to think about the possible dust bunnies behind the refrigerator. I tried not to think about anything except her insistent fingers pulling the crotch of my panties aside.

After we fucked I got up and straightened my skirt as if nothing had happened. It was almost like having sex with her had fixed me. Suddenly I had officially cheated and there was no going back. I was in love with my girlfriend and desired someone else. Someone I'd only met a few times in person but maybe was in love with. It was a lot easier to understand.

. . . . .

THAT NIGHT, JANEY wanted to stay home and fuck. But I wanted to get out and show her the city. I talked her into dinner, at least. "Come on. You haven't been here in forever. Let me show you around," I pleaded. I didn't want her entire visit to be spent in bed. I knew what effect that would have on my state of mind. And it wouldn't be a good one.

We got on the M train for a few stops and got off at Marcy. I took her across the Williamsburg Bridge on foot. "I grew up here, you know. You've only lived here two years. I know all this stuff," Janey complained as I dragged her around. It was 8 p.m. and still hot out. I'd changed into sandals for walking around but otherwise I was wearing the same clothes I had on while we were screwing on my kitchen floor. So was she. It was like having a secret.

I wanted to walk up to strangers and say, "Excuse

me, my girlfriend is in Indiana visiting her folks. I'm having an affair." I think this is what happens when you're raised Catholic. That desire to confess never really goes away. It's why I'm a bad liar. And the more I thought about it the more I wondered what I'd say to Cassy when she got home.

"I just want to show you the stuff I like," I replied. We held hands like a couple. At Delancey, we turned and headed for a ramen place I'd been to a few times. The pork was fatty and tender, swimming in thick salty broth. I liked hers better than mine and kept picking bits of cabbage from her bowl. Over sake she asked me if I was planning on telling Cassy about her.

"I think what I'm doing is compartmentalizing. It's like you and Cassy live in different spaces in my brain. You aren't going to live here. I'm not going to live in California. We can't be together. But when you left for Indonesia everything was so unfinished between us. I never really put you away like I wanted to. I'm in love with my girlfriend. I don't want to change my life." But then I didn't know if it was true. I guess maybe I wanted both. And that required changing things around. Cassy was so calm. She never got mad at me. She was reliable and smart. She was competent. She was so good.

We walked down Houston to the West Village. There was a Fassbinder retrospective at the Film Forum. And I begged her to see *The Marriage of Maria Braun* with me. "Please," I said. "Please? It's my favorite. And

Günther Kaufmann is in it! He's the crush-killer. He killed his agent by sitting on him. In real life. Like ten years ago or something."

We passed the time before it started with shots of whiskey in the bar down the street. "It's set in postwar Germany. It's depressing. But in a good way. The woman, Maria, thinks her husband is dead." I explained the plot to her while she absentmindedly stroked my arm. "And she takes on all these lovers kind of halfheartedly. Well, one guy, she sticks with for a while. The thing is, she was only married to her husband for one day. Then he got killed. OK, and then she doesn't have any money and she's a prostitute. And the doctor says something to her about how there's always penicillin. But she's really numb. She can't feel anything."

"I think I'm in love with you," Janey said. "Leave Cassy and I'll move to New York."

"And then she's having this affair with this American soldier. And the affair is going OK. They like each other. And he's really nice to her and brings food for her family and takes them on picnics and stuff. And so they are together like a couple. And then one day when they are about to get it on, her husband Hermann just shows up. It's so weird, he's not dead he's just standing there. And the soldier guy tries to protect Maria from Hermann but she grabs a vase and smacks the soldier over the head and kills him."

"I'm totally serious," Janey said in a weird, calm voice.

I pretended like I couldn't hear her.

"So then Hermann takes the blame for the murder and goes to prison. And Maria becomes this really shrewd businesswoman. And she has all these affairs. It's crazy. And she visits Hermann in prison and details her exploits and stuff. I never got that part. I think she loved Hermann. I don't know why she wanted him to go to prison. But she's so practical about love. She doesn't let it confuse her."

"What happens at the end?" Janey asked. "Do they finally get to be together? Does Hermann ever get out of jail? Are you going to fucking listen to what I'm saying? I said I'd move."

"OK, so then Hermann does get out of jail. I left out a whole part about this affair she had with her business partner Oswald. But you'll see. OK, so at the end, he gets out and it's like they are going to be a regular happy married couple. And Hermann is sitting in a chair watching the World Cup. And then Germany wins the World Cup. And there's an announcer saying in the background that Germany is something again."

"OK, how much longer is this story going to take? Are you going to avoid the topic of us all night long?" Janey was getting mad. Not so mad that she wouldn't play along. But I could hear the annoyance creeping into her voice.

"OK, so then guess what happens at the end?" I said excitedly.

"I can't wait," she sounded like a bitter Marlon

Brando in *Last Tango in Paris*. The part where Jeanne is talking about how much she loves her boyfriend. I think Jeanne has just said something about what her boyfriend does to make her fall in love with him. And Marlon Brando is so sarcastic. He's an asshole. Until the end that is. When he falls for her and she shoots him and tells the police he was a rapist.

"Well, the house blows up and they both die! And you don't really know whether Maria left the gas on purposefully or not. Maybe she killed them both so she wouldn't have to be a married woman."

. . . . .

JANEY AND I didn't have sex again after that first time on the floor. We spent the rest of the weekend together as friends. We shared the bed without touching. I wore pajamas. It wasn't that I felt like we were doing something wrong. It was more like I had made a decision. My pragmatic side had taken over once again. I think Janey realized I was mired in my life and content that way, so she didn't push it. She left that Monday. We kissed good-bye and hugged for a long time. Then we agreed to silence. No phone calls, no postcards. Nothing until the emotions had died down.

Cassy came home and I never told her anything. She asked me how my weekend was and if I had fun hanging out with my old friend. And I told her I did.

She talked about visiting her folks. About her new niece and her sister's frustration with having a toddler and an infant to take care of. She told me about her mom's diabetes and her dad's depression. And I kept silent. I looked at her and felt safe again. I felt like I'd put away some unfinished business and I could move on.

JESSIE, UNCONTROLLED

CHERYL MOCH

MY NEW BOSS was driving me crazy.

It wasn't the work. I'd been at the magazine for nearly ten years and I knew I could handle anything they threw at me. I was used to putting in long hours—no one was waiting for me at home anyway, not since my last girlfriend left me for the dubious charms of LA and the film industry. Kate had made a halfhearted effort to get me to move out there with her, but we both knew I wouldn't. Nothing could have gotten me to leave New York—I had the job I'd always dreamed of, as an editor at an upscale lifestyle magazine. Our relationship was probably headed for the rocks anyhow, and her departure was the most graceful way to end it.

By then, thanks to several promotions, I was able to handle payments on the condo with river views we shared in the Village. I had everything I needed, or so I thought, including an apartment scrubbed and tidied weekly by a gay male opera student moonlighting as a cleaning man. There was a vibrator in my night table, and I didn't need a map to find my own way between my legs. I would have said I was too busy to be lonely, but sometimes I woke up in the middle of the night sad to find there was no warm, fragrant body next to mine to curl up to.

I should have known my goose was cooked the first time I looked at my new boss, Jessie McCray. Because the office scuttlebutt was that she was involved with some Wall Street bond trader of blue-blooded lineage, I was expecting her to be a typical, straight Type A publishing exec—femmed and frilly and reeking of some expensive floral scent—in other words, not my type. So when she strode into the boardroom for her first meeting as editor-in-chief in a simply tailored Armani suit, her breasts playing peek-a-boo from the top of a crisp white cotton shirt, I was surprised. She was a little taller than me and, at thirty-four, a little older. Our boardroom is on the fiftieth floor of a midtown skyscraper and though the city and Central Park sparkled below, I found her blue eyes more dazzling than the view. She quickly took control of the meeting with a good-humored aggression that impressed me and everyone else in the room.

When I went up to introduce myself her grip on my hand seemed to linger a bit longer than was professionally necessary. She gazed right into my eyes and it was at that moment I should have just thrown in the towel. As she held my hand I could almost catch hold of her scent—but not quite. Sometimes I think I think with my nose—on some level, it's how I assess people. In corporate America many of the women douse themselves with expensive perfumes, fragrances that announce their arrival and departure, that continue to linger in the air once they're gone. But not this woman—her scent was subtle; in order to smell her, I'd have to get close. By the time I'd catch her scent, I'd have crossed the line. And at work, that can be dangerous, especially when the lady in question is your boss.

. . . . .

I'VE ALWAYS FELT that some degree of erotic tension is good at work. Makes the day pass more quickly. Makes late Sunday afternoons less unbearable. Tempts you back into the office each sleepy winter morning. The attraction between Jessie and me quickly escalated, or so it seemed to me. With each passing day I felt the pull to her strengthening, the air around us thicken. It was getting hard for me to think straight. As each story conference in her office ended, it got harder to just get up and walk out, I wanted so badly to reach out and touch her hair. I wanted to put my face to her neck and breathe her in.

I invented reasons to see her, stopping in her office

five or six times a day. If she seemed annoyed with me, which she sometimes did, I walked out, cheeks blazing, vowing to myself to leave her alone. But then she'd stop off at my office and stand really close by my side as we examined page layouts together, our arms brushing against each other. Still, she remained unapproachable. I began to think of her as cold, remote, overly formal. She didn't chitchat. I didn't know anything about her personal life. She could be very critical, of me and other staff members. If I made a mistake, or disagreed with her way of doing things, she could be mean. It seemed to me she didn't really smile, she just pulled back her lips and showed her teeth. She was always in control, of the magazine, of herself, of me. I wanted to see her lose that control. I wanted to see a glimpse into the real Jessie, her true self, no artifice. I wanted to hear a throaty scream, a deep moan, a sound that would surprise her, surprise me, as it escaped from her lips.

There were days when I thought, it's coming, I know it's coming. She is a fish and she is on my line. I must patiently reel her in. We exchanged playful e-mails. She praised my work, admired my new shoes. Then there were other days when I thought, she is a cat and I am her mouse. She will play with me, stroking with her sharp claws and leaving me for dead. Sometimes I just couldn't stand the frustration and I tried to avoid her altogether. I realized that my lips were getting chapped from wanting her, I was leaking vital nutrients, there was such exertion involved in not leaning in and touching her. I sometimes felt I had mastered the rotation of a large planet and could now make it spin backward, such was the will involved in not giving in to my desire to just reach out one small finger and trace the inside of her lips.

When I went home at night to my own bed I could still see her face as I closed my eyes and found my own pleasure.

Then, one day, there was a crisis at the magazine. At the very last minute before we went to press, a long piece we were going to run had to be dropped, and we were suddenly short several pages. We had no choice but to work late into the night, writing and editing, looking at artwork and layouts. One by one worn-out assistants were sent home for the night. Finally, it was just me, Jessie, and the art director. Jessie had taken off her jacket sometime during the night. She was wearing a sleeveless shirt and I was distracted to find that she had rippling arm muscles. Her imperious ways were getting to me as the night wore on, but so was her body. I disagreed with a decision of hers and we squabbled so intensely that the art director, listening to us, said, "What's with you two?" Minutes later, we were leaning over a layout when we got so lost in each others eyes that the art director actually said, "Ladies, could I have your attention?"

Finally, we were finished. The art director couldn't get away from us fast enough. He murmured his good nights and ran. I went into my office to quickly gather up my things and walked down the hall to Jessie's office. She didn't look at me. Silently we walked together down the hall to the elevator. The lights at that hour were dimmed in the hallways and it was strange standing with her in the semidarkness waiting for the elevator, bathed in the red glow of the exit sign. I wanted to say something to her but I didn't know what. Finally the elevator arrived and we stepped in. Both of us reached for the lobby button and our fingers touched. She grabbed my hand and pulled me toward her. Her tongue was down my throat before we descended one floor. It was a fifty-story free fall and as far as I was concerned, I would have stayed in that elevator forever.

When we got to the lobby and the doors opened we managed to pull apart. The security guard barely glanced up at us as we approached and he told us to sign out. I was breathing heavily as I reached for the pen, and my hands were shaking a little. Jessie told me to sign her out too. She kept walking, swept into the night through the revolving door. I put the pen down and rushed to catch up with her.

Shiny black limos are a common sight on midtown streets at night. They sit at the curb, faithful as little dogs, waiting for big executives to be released from work. Jessie was provided this luxury when she worked late—she was, after all, the editor-in-chief. She was just climbing into the backseat of a limo as I exited the building. I couldn't wait to cozy up next to her in the comfortable car and slip my hands down her shirt. But to my astonishment, she got in, slammed the door shut, then rolled down the window.

"Sorry, Lina," she said as I ran up to the car, "but I'm going uptown."

Then she took off. Just like that, just as cold as ice. Leaving me alone on the emptied city street throbbing with desire for her as I watched the car disappear. It was a warm spring evening, but I was suddenly chilled and pulled my jacket tight around me. I could still feel her lips hard on mine. Moreover I could finally smell her, her scent had rubbed off on my clothes, on my hands, a rich buttery scent, mixed with ginger. I breathed her in, heartbroken and confused. I wanted to throttle her at that moment just as I wanted to make love to her. I had never felt so aroused, so frustrated, so heartbroken and abandoned. Her face, those blue eyes echoed insistently through my mind.

I knew I couldn't go home, not in that condition. I thought of tracking her to her house. I knew where she lived, but maybe her bond trader boyfriend would be there. Anyway, she had a doorman, and I couldn't bear the humiliation of not being let up, of some uniformed man saying Sorry miss, you can't go up there.

I thought of going to a bar—there were a couple of women's bars in my neighborhood and I generally could find someone to go home with, but easy anonymous sex was not what I wanted. For as long as it took to descend fifty stories I thought I was finally going to penetrate deep into the mysteries of my boss, not just her body but her heart. I was going to scale the high fence of her defenses and get to see the real Jess. But now I was alone in the midtown street, skyscrapers rising up all around me, the luminous night light of the city making the whole world seem like a black and white movie. The sound of the passing cars and taxis echoed against the buildings. In the distance I heard the groans of a garbage truck.

. . . . .

WHEN PEOPLE THINK about New York they generally think about a city of steel and granite rising into the sky, lights blazing 24/7, the rush and the bustle. But there was something else I loved about the city: that it lay sprawled out against the sea, and that for a couple of bucks the subway took you from the glamour of midtown Manhattan to the shores of the Atlantic. Back when Kate announced she was leaving me and I saw the future I'd envisioned for us vanish, I took my heartache to the beach and offered it to the pounding surf. I remembered that the ride on the Coney Island–bound B train had soothed me then, and after Jessie pulled away I went to the corner subway entrance and descended the stairs. Soon the steady rocking of the subway car was pulling me to the sea.

Outside of Manhattan, the train ran above ground and I watched as the city grew less congested, apartment buildings replaced by little houses with gardens and driveways, the grittiness of the central city tamed by domestic order. I saw myself reflected in the window of the train as I thought about the elevator ride. She had pulled me to her. Her desire for me had been evident. She'd kissed my throat whispering my name, over and over again, as she pressed her body to mine, ran her hands through my hair, down my back, and onto my ass.

And then? She ran off. *Sorry, Lina, but I'm going uptown.* Oh, we were going in different directions all right—she went straight to her boyfriend and all the comforts and privilege of her life with him. She was at war with her own desire, that's what I thought, and I was a casualty of that war.

I got out of the subway at the last stop and ran over to the beach. I took off my shoes and the sand massaged my feet as I walked to the water. Behind me the skeleton of the roller coaster seemed like the ruins of some ancient temple. The moon, high now in the sky, shone on the water. I took the salty air deep into my lungs. The churning and turbulence of the waves matched my own. The sound of their crashing on the shore drowned out my sobbing. I called out her name, over and over again, I stood at the ocean's edge and all of the months of pent up frustration, hope, and desire poured out of me. I would never get to unwrap the prize, feel the texture of her skin, listen to Jessie uncontrolled as I brought her to climax. I would never hold her in my arms, coax her into relaxing and love her into loving me.

I had played that risky game of office romance and I had lost.

And to add to my misery, I fully expected her to fire me when I returned to work the next morning.

But I never got to work the next morning. Sometime during the night, I sat down on the beach and must have fallen asleep because the sun was rising over the Atlantic when I woke up. There was no one else around. My hair was filled with sand, my clothes were creased and dirty. I could feel that my eyes were puffy. I turned around and got back on the train, fighting sleep all the way back to the Village.

When I got to my apartment, the light was blinking on my telephone. I ignored it and headed straight for the shower, dropping my clothes along the way. The hot water felt good as it washed away the night. I was wrapped in my white terry bathrobe and my hair was still wet as I stood in my kitchen, trying to decide whether to brew a pot of coffee or just get into bed and pull the covers over my head when the phone rang. It was Jessie.

"Thank God you're OK," she said. " I've been calling you all night . . . Where were you, why haven't you been answering your phone?"

I didn't think she had earned the right to any information about me or my whereabouts.

"What is it you want?" I asked her.

"I've been in a panic trying to find you. I realized as

soon as I pulled away that I'd made a terrible mistake. I had the driver turn around and we tried to find you. I spent the night in the coffee shop around the corner from your house. Can I come over?"

I was still in my bathrobe when she got there, and the pot of coffee I'd put on was brewing. It wasn't easy for her to explain how terrified she was of her own feelings for me. I didn't make it easy for her, and why should I? I wanted to make sure—really sure—that she wasn't going to bolt again. She'd been up all night and she looked bedraggled. I had never seen her like that before. I had never seen her look scared before. We drank coffee and I let her pour her heart out to me, about what the last several months had been like for her, wanting me and not wanting to want me. I made her sit across the room from me as we talked—no touching. It was the last time I had to resist her like that.

It's been six years since that day, and we're still happily together. She's still a brat sometimes, willful and impossible and controlling but she's also interesting and smart and funny. I got her to move downtown. And she was never my boss again—I handed in my resignation as I undressed her that first morning. She used her connections in publishing to get me a new job—I'm editor-in-chief now of a rival publication. So I'm the boss at work, but when I get home, well, with Jessie that's always negotiable.

THE FABLE OF THE NEW YORK MINUTE

LYNNE JAMNECK

*It is a miracle that New York works at all. The
whole thing is implausible.*

—E.B. WHITE

IT HAPPENED SLOWLY, but quite obviously,
which caught me off guard. And I'm not talking days
or months either.

In the past I have fallen in love rather quickly; an
unfortunate character flaw, according to those who
know me. I can be careless with my emotions, but
I guess you can't change who you are. Trying to is a
misguided attempt that tends to make life difficult,
more so than it already is.

I grew up all over Staten Island. My parents were
divorced when I was twelve, and for the next few years

we moved around according to the tax rate and the dictate of my mother's salary. Those were good times. We could always laugh. It was tough sometimes, but we were never hungry and never cold. We even ate enough sugar to warrant trips to the dentist.

People have the impression that the island is all blue-collar and grit. While we certainly know how to graft, there's much more across the Hudson than meets the eye. The place is littered with centers focusing on the arts: theater companies, museums, and musical institutions like the Staten Island Barbershop Chorus. There's even an archeological society. Manhattanites like to look down on us, but only because they have taller buildings.

Chloe Riddick is my best friend. In primary school she gave Mike Dupont a bloody nose after he stole my Reese's Pieces. We've been inseparable ever since. Chloe's a high school teacher at Notre Dame Academy. She always jokes that it's probably the closest she'll ever get to Paris. She teaches theology in the school's advanced placement program. I've always found that quietly curious, since the woman doesn't seem to have a religious bone in her body.

I was a closet intellectual long before I ever knew about Chloe's aspirations to teach. Chloe was always the cool one, even if she didn't try to be. I only found out later that she had these incredibly complex thought processes running through her mind. When we were twenty-one, she told me she had a need to understand religion. I asked her why try to understand something that has no logic to it? She said because she didn't want to become a psychiatrist. I had no idea it was either one or the other. Chloe liked making good-natured but merciless fun of me and my Bachelor's in art, but only because she knew it had the desired effect. I knew she was just teasing; Chloe probably wasn't aware of her real motives most of the time.

. . . . .

THE STATEN ISLAND Museum is my home. Where I live is my apartment.

I've been the assistant curator at the museum for five years. I get to look at fine works of art from all over the world every day, and I still can't believe my luck. People think that the idea of a "dream job" is a myth, but I'm here to prove them wrong.

Chloe's always dragging me onto the ferry and into Manhattan whenever she gets the chance. Sometimes I think she's seen *Working Girl* one time too many. I'm one to talk: I had a crush on Sigourney Weaver that stood as high as the Chrysler Building. Yeah, sorta like Ms. Weaver—tall.

Despite having a projected population of almost 500,000, Staten Island is regularly referred to as "the forgotten borough." It has four sisters that are much more famous: Queens, Brooklyn, Bronx, and Manhattan. Personally, I find it comforting that the

island is slightly removed from its more popular coun-
terparts. Looking out at the Manhattan skyline at night
from the ferry is a breathtaking sight. Somehow you
always feel like you're in a Woody Allen film. It can
even make a sometimes-dunce like me feel like a true
woman-of-the-world.

I love jazz. That's why I let Chloe drag me into the
midst of the glitz come weekends. Chloe doesn't need
to love anything in order to enjoy it. She's different from
me in that way. There are times when I wish I was more
like her, but she always tells me otherwise. Chloe says
if we weren't so innately different we'd never be able to
get along.

· · · · ·

CHLOE HAD A girlfriend when we were seventeen.
I remember being bowled over by her balls for being
so blatant about it. Her name was Janis, but Chloe used
to call her Ian because she looked so much like you-
know who.

Janis was cool. She was so obviously queer, and she was
butch in a way that was devastatingly alluring. I still think
that some of my adult mannerisms came from Chloe's
first girlfriend: the way Janis cradled Chloe protectively
in the crook of her arm; the way her feet always seemed
firmly planted on the ground; and the confident swagger
in her hips as she strutted down Fifth Avenue like she
owned the goddamn place. I knew without a doubt then

that I wanted to be like Janis, I was just too young and full of brass to realize why.

Janis was crazy about Bruce Springsteen. When I think back to those days, the three of us in my blue, beat-up Chevy crossing the Brooklyn Bridge to the sound of The Boss, I still get shivers up and down my arms. There were lights everywhere and possibility pungent in the air. I can still remember the way Chloe smelled; a heady, future-excited mix of youth and burgeoning adulthood, opening like a promise waiting to be fulfilled.

I realize now, as I huddle myself inside my black trench coat, waiting for the ferry to take me back to the island, there must be a reason why I remember certain things with such peculiar detail. Like the dark fire in Chloe's eyes when she'd looked at me when we were seventeen, Janis' arm around her while the butch girl laughed at the comedians in Central Park.

. . . . .

CHRISTMAS WAS ONE week away. Both Chloe and I had been single for what seemed an inordinate amount of time. We're pretty good at making fun of each other's love lives. Sometimes it's easier to make peace with something if you can laugh at it.

We were splurging on dinner at The Tavern on the Green. It was only a pretentious thing to do if you were a tourist, and besides, the Shiraz there was worth committing a felony for. The only real problem was how to decide from the eight different menus what you wanted to eat.

I'd been staring at the snowflakes drifting down slowly on Central Park when I realized Chloe was rambling about something. I stopped her verbal train of thought and asked, "You broke up with her because you couldn't understand what she was saying?"

Chloe's salad fork stopped halfway to her mouth before returning to her plate. "The woman was a linguist's nightmare."

"How bad could it have been? This *is* New York, after all."

Chloe interpreted with an affected accent. "I was toy teen when my mudder got remarried. She now lives in Stat Nigh Lynn, but sometimes I think she really misses New Yawk. She's originally from Long Guy Lynn."

"Wow. That's quite something."

"Tell me about it." Chloe stabbed her coleslaw. "How did your blind date go?"

"It didn't. Well, *I* didn't."

"You didn't go?"

I pitched my shoulders before she could say anything else. "I don't know what an art curator and a fireman—firewoman, whatever—would have in common."

"Your loss. I hear they're really great in bed. Must be all that hosing practice."

I snorted and Shiraz sprayed out of my nose.

"I saw Ian in the newspaper last week."

My heart skipped like a silly school girl's. "Janis?"

Chloe nodded, chewing salad. "Uh huh. She's the lead singer for some band or other I get the feeling I'm supposed to have heard of. Anyway, I'm happy for her. It's what she always wanted."

I swallowed more wine. "Do you ever miss her?"

Chloe's dark eyes watched me. I looked away and cut my steak.

"No. Not as much as I miss that time; the feeling of it. Like anything was possible."

I felt small suddenly. I couldn't look at Chloe. So I chewed my steak, which was very well done, and waited until she'd gone to the bathroom before I ordered more wine and drank down half a glass before she came back.

. . . . .

PART OF THE magic of living on Staten Island is taking the ferry from the Whitehall Terminal in Lower Manhattan back across the spreading Hudson River. There's something both tragic and foot-stompingly regal about the Manhattan skyline receding.

From the deck, you have access to a faultless view of Ellis Island and the Statue of Liberty. The skyscrapers and bridges of Lower Manhattan withdraw gradually as the ferry pulls away from Whitehall, and come back into focus again when you approach from Staten Island.

Chloe came to stand next to me, her presence a reassurance that I've always needed through the years.

She handed me a plastic cup of coffee. "Remember Mike Dupont?"

"That redheaded dwarf who always tried to steal my candy?"

Chloe sipped her coffee. A smile bled reminiscence around her full lips. "He got busted for running a chop shop in Queens. Can you believe he phoned me to bail him out?"

I looked at her, incredulous. "He did?"

"Sure. People think because they live in New York they can do anything without explanation."

"You mean, New Yawk?"

"Of course I do."

I wondered, as we drank our coffee why Chloe had been talking about the past so much of late. Maybe it was because she would turn thirty a week after Christmas; maybe it was just a matter of reflection.

I was careful. I didn't want her to notice the way I glanced at her reflection in the ferry window. Chloe was slightly taller than me, with hair so dark it would put a crow to shame. Sometimes I thought that I could sense something in her, an emptiness that she never talked about. She always changed the subject when I tried to probe. All I knew was that there were eight million people in New York City, and out of all those, Chloe was the only one I'd never tire of. To lose her friendship would be a deep, dark blow.

I suddenly felt Chloe's hand grip my wrist, the way she'd last done when we were almost caught fooling around in Central Park. It had only been one kiss, a brief but tangible moment.

Chloe pulled me, her smile brilliant as she turned to me and said, "Washda Closendaws."

. . . . .

IT WAS CHRISTMAS Eve. All of Staten Island was nestled in an icy white blanket.

Chloe and I drove home, suddenly quiet after she'd once again pulled me so gleefully from the ferry. It was getting dark. We passed the familiar sign that read WELCOME TO STATEN ISLAND, EST. 1661. Ahead was the toll plaza. *Reduce speed* another yellow sign warned. I watched the road codes slip past, aware of Chloe's silence. Several cars were already lined up in front of us.

Both of us suddenly didn't seem to want to talk. It was an uncomfortable silence.

Neither of us would be spending time with family. Mine couldn't afford to fly in to New York, and Chloe didn't have any family to speak of. She was always talking about a homophobic cousin somewhere, but she only knew him well enough to be able to make fun of him. Her parents died in a car crash when she was nineteen, almost twelve years ago.

Chloe broke the silence. "I wonder how many songs

there are with the words 'New York' in the title." She was looking out the passenger window, back across the Hudson.

" 'New York, New York'."

" 'New York State of Mind'."

" 'Fairytale of New York'."

" 'Autumn in New York'."

" 'New York's in Love'."

" 'The Peking King and the New York Queen'."

" 'Fork New York'."

" 'Daddy Don't Live in that New York City No More'."

" 'An Englishman in New York'."

" 'I Can't See New York'."

" 'I Feel Safe in New York City'."

Chloe looked at me with a frown. "You think anyone ever sings about Staten Island?"

"There's one called 'Staten Island Baby', but I have no idea who the artist is."

"Black 47."

We drove through the toll. I waited until I could turn off, then asked, "How do you get from popular music to the blackest year of the Irish potato famine?"

"The band. 'Staten Island Baby'? Their name was Black 47."

"Aha."

Chloe had a thin trickle of Irish in her blood. Her family's family was originally from Galway. She can say 'fuck' in Gaelic.

Silence settled again. As I turned onto the street I'd been living on for almost ten years I could no longer disregard the nature of the tension between us. I accepted it then, and I felt Chloe did, too. That's why we'd talked about songs with 'New York' in the title; as if it was something completely new, a guessing game we haven't played countless times before.

. . . . .

WITHIN HALF AN hour I had a fire going and Chloe was swaying to Louis Armstrong in my living room. She really was a good dancer, but she always said that jazz gave her two left feet.

The Christmas tree glowed. If I had chestnuts, you could be sure I'd know what to do with them.

"Where the hell is my gift?" I asked loudly above the music, checking on the roast in the oven.

Chloe didn't stop moving. She pointed to the tree. "Right there." She smiled at me, and there was a certain intimacy in the gesture. I was sure I misinterpreted it. I'd better take it easy on the eggnog.

"That one small little box?"

"Well, where's mine then?" She kept dancing, twirling.

"How can you miss it?" The big green box was tied with a white ribbon. It was a DVD entertainment system. I just couldn't bear the thought of Chloe watching anymore movies on VHS.

I finished in the kitchen and poured two more glasses of rum-spiked eggnog. We watched Christmas specials on television and made fun of the overblown, sugary sentimentality. Both of us overestimated our capacity for hard liquor. We fell asleep on the couch before midnight, arms wrapped around one another. I slept without dreaming.

· · · · ·

WHEN I WOKE up the next morning I was still on the couch, huddled cozily beneath a blanket. A shaft of light cut across my feet through the open curtain. The fire had long since gone out, but the room was still warm. I smelled Chloe on my skin before I recognized the aroma of coffee drifting through from the kitchen. A jazzy version of "Jingle Bells" swung softly in the background.

Chloe appeared in the doorway, a mug of steaming coffee in each hand. *She's beautiful. Look at her sexy bed-hair.*

I sat up self-consciously. Chloe wavered. The silence bound us.

Finally she said, "What did you put in that eggnog?"

I smirked. "If memory serves, you were the one who kept tipping the bottle of Bacardi in the bowl every time you thought I wasn't looking." I took the mug she held out to me and dared a small sip, looking at Chloe next to me on the couch from above the rim.

She stood up, too quickly, spilling coffee on herself.

"Whoopsie." I laughed nervously and raced to get a cloth from the kitchen. Chloe didn't even seem to notice the hot coffee. Two red blotches were already forming on her legs. I got down on my knees between Chloe's legs to wipe down her skin, even though all the coffee had dripped to the floor already.

"You don't have to do that," Chloe said. Her palm brushed the top of my hand when she tried to take the kitchen cloth from me. I grabbed but caught only her fingers, held them tight and as I scooted closer to her, still on my knees, Chloe bent down to kiss me.

Like a lit match, we were on fire. Chloe's arms were around me, I felt her hands touching my neck and then she pulled me up against her, the warmth of our bodies infusing. I could feel her respond to me, years of uncertainty and restraint coming loose. Her tongue was in my mouth, warm and hot. I thought I was dreaming.

"Merry Christmas," Chloe stumbled when we came up for air. I didn't dare open my mouth. We looked at one another for a moment and I could still recognize the seventeen-year-old with the dark eyes in Chloe's face. I felt as inexperienced as she looked. But the heat between us overrode everything.

We made love on the couch, moved to the floor, and eventually ended up in my bed, spent and slick and hungry, oblivious of the yuletide. I thought I knew Chloe, but I realized, again, that even best friends have secrets. Lovers, however, have few.

It's silly, when I think about it. Neither Chloe nor I had ever backed away from anything in our lives. Sometimes we even did things that others considered irresponsible. "We chisel our demons into angels," Chloe always said. As I lie in bed now, Chloe protectively in the crook of my arm and my fingers tracing her hair, I listen. There's nothing but our collective breathing, evening out. The rattle and shake in my chest is gone. It's Christmas. I've been in love for seventeen years. I guess sometimes these things take a little time.

TOSSING ASIDES

YOLANDA WALLACE

HER NAME WAS Adrian. She was thirty-seven or thirty-eight. I wasn't sure which. Thirtysomething, but just barely. She was an art history professor at Columbia. At least, that was her day job. She was also an artist who specialized in abstract landscapes, images that never quite came into focus no matter how close to or far away from the canvas one stood. Those who can, do. Those who can't, teach. Those with too much time on their hands do both.

I was a cater-waiter. Cater-*waitress*, to be exact. I was twenty-nine. Of that, I was certain. Twentysomething, but just barely. I specialized in handing out free drinks and hors d'oeuvres to the pretentious. I shouldn't pass judgment on them. The pretentious, not the crudités. Some of them tipped very well. The pretentious, not the crudités. They should have tipped well. After all, they could afford to write a check equal to two years of my salary just to have a pretty picture to hang over the john. They could afford to commission an original piece, then send it back because it was too blue or too red or just didn't match the décor. They could afford to be assholes. And not all of them were assholes. Some of them used their expensive Ivy League educations to become witty, not catty. Except for Crawford Butler, the obnoxious art critic for the *Times*. I tried to avoid him, but he was hard to miss. He was the one who kept grabbing champagne cocktails with one hand and my butt with the other.

Adrian caught my eye after my third close encounter with Mr. Grab Ass. Surrounded by students, fans, hangers-on, and a cadre of reporters, she gave me a sympathetic smile and a "What can I do?" shrug. I smiled back, but I knew there was nothing either of us could do except grin and bear it. She was having her first exhibition in four years. The company I worked for was supplying the catering. Her people couldn't (wouldn't) say anything to Butler because they didn't want to risk a bad review. My people couldn't (wouldn't) say anything to him because they didn't want to risk losing such a high-paying gig when the economy was still so uncertain.

I worked for Party to Go-Go, a catering company that also provided party planning. As it said on the side of our vans, we brought the food and the fun. And, unfortunately, we also cleaned up afterward. That's what Jason Keenan and I were doing—or supposed to be doing—when Adrian caught us.

Jason was our bartender. His drinks were unspectacular and strictly by the book, but his tip jar was always overflowing because he was model handsome while somehow managing to remain nonthreateningly sexy. Twenty-one, he wanted to be a stockbroker when he grew up. As crazy as Wall Street was post-9/11, I wasn't going anywhere near the markets, but it was his dream, not mine. I kept my savings—what precious little there was of them—in a jar in my closet the way my grandparents used to.

"How did you make out tonight?" Jason asked, sweeping up the remnants of that night's party. The theme had been the Roaring '20s in honor of the centerpiece of Adrian's show, a sprawling work titled *London Fog, 1926.*

I told Jason about my hands-on experience with Crawford Butler. "What did you do," I asked, "put Viagra in his drink instead of bitters?"

"Next time, I'll use saltpeter, okay?"

"No, next time, just take a whizz in the bathtub gin."

"Deal." He dumped the mess we'd swept up into the trash. Then he rolled the heavy plastic can to the dumpster out back.

Leaning on my broom, I stared up at *London Fog.* If I approached it from the right angle, I could just make out Big Ben and the Tower of London. And there, under a hazy streetlamp, was an early version of a double decker bus. Behind it, a precursor to those cool old-fashioned cabs that still prowled the British streets. The painting made me nostalgic for a city I'd never visited, for an era I'd never experienced firsthand. Ten feet high and fourteen feet wide, the painting also made me feel small. That word, however, could not have been used to describe the price tag. The list price was six figures; it had sold for almost seven. Little red dots were affixed to the title cards of each piece in the show, meaning that all twelve paintings had been sold. The exhibition would go on for another month, but it had become simply that—an exhibition. "Look, but don't touch," those little red dots said. "These belong to someone else."

Upon his return, Jason whistled in admiration at the price tag and rambled on for a while about the appreciating investment value of art. "If you did it right, you could double or even triple your initial investment, but that's a lot of money to dole out for some paint splattered on a canvas."

"No," I corrected him, "Jackson Pollock splattered. This is—"

"Eight hundred thousand dollars worth of smearing," he supplied.

"Actually," a voice behind us chimed in, "with the canvas and the paint, it's only $1,000 worth of smearing. The rest is for coming up with the title. The inspiration was free, but it is very hard work coming up with those self-important titles, don't you agree?"

We whirled around, praying we wouldn't see the person we knew would be standing there. Adrian had stayed behind to dot some *i*'s and cross some *t*'s with the gallery owners after the showing. Since they'd made a killing, everyone was in a good mood—we hoped.

I looked into her eyes. Intense and Paul Newman blue, they had beckoned me from the covers of countless magazines. I had read three of the dozens of articles about her. One had said she was gay, one bisexual, one married with three kids. I didn't know which reporter had gotten it right, but I hoped I hadn't been wrong in assuming that those eyes belonged to a woman with a sense of humor. If not, they belonged to a woman who most assuredly could make life very miserable for me.

"I'm sorry," I apologized. "We were just—" I turned to Jason for reassurance, but he'd disappeared faster than a Cheshire cat and he hadn't even bothered to leave his grin behind as evidence. I was alone with her. "*I*," I amended, "was just—"

She held up her hands. Heavy silver cuffs adorned her wrists—they reminded me of Wonder Woman's magic bracelets—but her fingers were bare. So much for the married-with-children story. "It's all right," she said. She spoke with the uncertain accent peculiar to those who traveled too much. "I'm used to it. If I were that thin-skinned, I would have changed professions a long time ago." She extended her hand. "Adrian de Laclos," she introduced unnecessarily.

"Jude Applegate," I said, shaking her hand. My real

name was Judith, but no one had ever called me that. I'd never been a Judith. Or a Judy, for that matter. Always Jude.

"Pleased to meet you, Jude." She bent and picked up a spangle that had fallen off of my dress. I couldn't wait to get home and get out of my costume. I was more comfortable in a sweatshirt and jeans, not fishnets and a sequined flapper outfit. I didn't recognize myself in the getup; she probably wouldn't have recognized me out of it. Then again, she was a minimalist. She was accustomed to stripping away the layers in order to find what was essential. "We have a mutual friend in Mr. Crawford Butler, I believe?" she asked, pocketing the spangle. As a souvenir of the occasion or as inspiration for a future work? I didn't dare ask.

"Unfortunately, yes."

"I'm terribly sorry about that. If there's anything I can do to make it up to you—"

"*He* should apologize, not you."

"Even so, I feel responsible. The unpleasantness occurred at my show."

"It was your show, but not your fault. Besides, if he and I cross paths again, he will be the one to regret it, not me." I winced at the grammatical error, but it was too late to correct it without drawing attention to it. Maybe someday someone will see fit to invent verbal Wite-Out. That's a stock I would buy without hesitation.

She looked at me and I felt as if we'd connected,

then she asked, "Are you almost done here?" and I was reminded that I was only the hired help.

"Almost." There was probably something I hadn't done, but nothing that came immediately to mind.

"Then would you like to have a cup of coffee with me?"

I didn't drink coffee—I was hyper enough without the jolt of caffeine—but I was sure coffee was just an excuse. She felt guilty about not coming to my defense earlier and she wanted to make it up to me. She couldn't have been asking me out just to go out, could she?

"Coffee black or coffee *and*?" I indicated the people hanging around the fringes of the room.

"Black, if that's okay." She cocked her head to one side like an inquisitive child. "Or do you have someone waiting at home who would take offense to that?"

I gave her points for remembering to ask the question rather than assuming I'd go out with her no matter what the answer was just because of who she was. "No one human." The only person waiting at home for me was my cat. A calico, half her face was orange and the other half was brown. I called her TB, short for Two-Faced Bitch. She lived up to the name, too—she'd bite the hand that fed it, then turn around and lick it.

"In that case, is your calendar free or do you have another more pressing engagement scheduled for tonight? A rendezvous at a speakeasy, perhaps?"

Apparently, she *really* liked the costume. "Actually, I do have plans." I was pleased to see disappointment register in those blue eyes. "I have a secret assignation lined up with Jodie Foster. We're going to thumb our noses at Prohibition." I'd rented *Flightplan* four days before, but I hadn't had a chance to watch the movie and the DVD was due back the next day.

"Do you have a lookout, someone to flash you the secret signal in case the police arrive unexpectedly?"

"No, we hadn't thought of that."

"Poor party planning on your part. I should tell your boss."

"You wouldn't want to get me in trouble, would you?"

"Actually, yes, I would," she said, "but not with your boss."

I still didn't know which team she played for, but I enjoyed playing her game. Feeling more than a spark of electricity between us, I surged ahead. "You could join us, if you like. Lookout isn't a very well-paying job, but the incentive package is pretty good."

"Would I have full medical and dental?"

"That's negotiable after your first performance review."

Her eyes twinkled like the nursery rhyme. "I'm afraid I'm out of practice. I wouldn't want that to count against me."

"I'll be gentle, I promise."

Her smile turned into a devilish grin. "I don't like things gentle," she said in a whisper as sweet as honeyed whiskey. "If we're going to do this, please remember that." Then, louder, "Shall I bring the derringer or the Tommy gun?"

"Just bring you," I said, struggling to keep up. I was the one who was out of practice. My last girlfriend and I had broken up two years before when she'd left me for a pierced and tattooed talking head on MTV. I'd dipped my toe into the dating pool during the time between and I'd even waded in up to my knees once or twice, but I hadn't dived in and tested the deep end. With Adrian, I felt like I could get in over my head if I weren't careful. "I'll take care of everything else."

"That's the best offer I've had all day." I handed her a card that contained all my pertinent information—address, phone number, shoe size, favorite color. "Give me time to say goodnight to some people and I'll see you as soon as I can, Jude."

I loved the way my name sounded coming off her tongue. I wanted to come off her tongue. She turned to go, but I stopped her. "Tell me one thing first."

"Is this something I make a habit of doing? No. As a general rule, I don't sleep with students or have wild nights on the town with flappers and Ivy League-educated actresses."

"That wasn't my question, but thank you," I said, trying not to laugh. I was right—she was a woman with a sense of humor. "What I'd like to know is what would you like for breakfast?" So much for being careful. Her blue eyes flashed. It was a bad habit of mine—planning for the future before the present had passed. I'd either sealed the deal or broken our handshake agreement. "With a comment like that, Jude, I don't know whether to slap you or kiss you."

"I'd prefer it if you kissed me," I said with a shrug and a smile, "but that's just me."

She leaned in close to me, shattering the traditional three-foot social barrier, the amount of space you're supposed to maintain during a conversation with someone you don't know very well. Her lips swept past mine, brushed my cheek, and nestled against my ear. "Soon," she promised.

She was wearing some flowing outfit that I didn't know how to describe. It wasn't a muumuu or a caftan. It was more like a sari, yards and yards of material carefully wound and draped just so. I probably could have unraveled her like the mummy if I'd known the proper technique. Now knowing the proper technique, I turned into Crawford Butler—I grabbed her and held on. So much for personal space. I'd just met her and I already didn't want to let her get away. "How soon?" I pressed, inhaling her scent.

"Will you be counting the minutes?" she murmured in my ear.

"I already am."

She freed herself from me. "Give me forty-five minutes," she said, backing away. "Thirty if I'm lucky. Fifteen if I'm rude."

"And less than that?"

"Only if I break every rule known to man. Which

I have been known to do, by the way," she tossed over her shoulder. "Don't wait for me," she cautioned, "but expect me. I *will* be there, Jude."

The difference between waiting for someone and expecting someone, as I came to find out, is this: when you're waiting for someone, it's within the boundaries of an agreed-upon time frame; when you're expecting someone, time goes out the window.

· · · · ·

I GRABBED A quick shower and began to wait for her. Fifteen minutes passed. I queued the DVD. Thirty minutes passed. I curled up on the couch to watch some TV until she arrived. Forty-five minutes passed. I got up to feed TB. An hour went by. I tried to convince myself that, technically, she was only fifteen minutes late. After ninety minutes, I tried to convince myself that she was going to show up at all. After two hours, I reluctantly gave up and started the movie without her. I hadn't expected her to be early—she'd been in too expansive a mood for that—but I hadn't expected her to be egregiously late, either. Or stand me up altogether. She'd seemed too considerate to do something like that.

She rang the buzzer right after the opening credits rolled. I was ecstatic that she'd showed up, but I didn't want to let her off easy. I pardoned her the second I heard her voice—I didn't live in the best neighborhood and I'd been worried something had happened to her on the way to my apartment—but I had to at least give the appearance of making her work for my forgiveness.

"Yes?" I said noncommittally into the intercom next to my front door as TB circled my ankles.

"I could be flippant and say, 'What did I miss?'" Adrian said into the intercom downstairs on the front stoop.

"Jodie left. She said she couldn't wait any longer. Something about a 4 a.m. wake-up call."

"That's too bad. I could be cocky and say, 'I was trying to decide what you should make me for breakfast.'"

"Kitchen's closed," I retorted.

"I figured that. I could be tactful and say, 'I was unavoidably detained.'"

"I don't like that one."

"Neither do I. I could cut my losses, tuck my tail between my legs and go home."

She sounded serious. I tried not to sound desperate. "I don't like that one, either," I said as matter-of-factly as I could.

"Neither do I." She sounded relieved. "I could remind you that I'm an artist and I can't be counted on to be dependable."

"Then I'd have to remind you that you're also a professor and the two sides counteract each other."

"Not necessarily, but since I'm already behind, I'll concede the argument anyway. I could be forceful and say, 'Let me in.' "

"Not by the hair of my chinny chin chin. It's *my* apartment, remember?"

"Quite right. I could be remorseful—which I am, by the way—and say, 'There are no words to express how much I regret having to apologize to you twice in one night.' "

"Getting better, but verging on treacle."

"I could be romantic and say, 'I never believed in love at first sight until now.' "

"Beside the point and heading straight into Hallmark card territory."

"I could be responsible and say, 'I went out with some of my students, I lost track of time and I'm deeply embarrassed about it.' "

I pondered that one. I could have ended the game right there, but I was having too much fun. She excited my mind as well as my body. My synapses overruled my hormones. "Getting there."

"Or I could be honest and say, 'I haven't been this excited about something—*someone*—in quite a while and it took me this long to calm myself down enough to come over here.' What would you say to that?"

That one surprised me, but in a pleasant way. I took a moment to gather myself. "I could say, 'What took you so long?' "

"Too confrontational," she replied, turning the tables on me.

"I could say, 'Are all dates with you this verbose?' "

"No, quite a few involve comfortable silences, but too cutting."

"I could say, 'Where have you been all my life?'"

"Too 1930's romantic drama."

"I could say, 'Ditto.'"

"Too Patrick Swayze in *Ghost*."

"I could say, 'Come up and see me sometime.'"

"Too Mae West. Fortunately, I like Mae West."

"I could say, 'I think I love you.'"

"Same here, but multiple fouls on that one. Too sudden. Too David Cassidy. Too Hugh Grant in *Four Weddings and a Funeral*."

"Then I guess I'll just say, 'Hurry up. You're missing the movie.'"

"I like that one."

"So do I."

AFTER THE RAIN

RACHEL ROSENBERG

FOR A MOMENT, Becca stood in the rain and stared up at the sky with a frown. "Oh, c'mon," she mumbled and then ran down the steps of the nearest subway. Her brown hair felt heavy and was plastered to her head, long bangs in her face like a dripping wet wall that blocked her sight. She parted it with damp fingers and then wiped her hands against the legs of her jeans. The jeans themselves were soaked in patches, like parts of her body had been glued into them with the kind of liquid glue she'd used in art classes when she was ten years old.

She had been walking with Cullen, in and out of various used bookstores, stopping at each sidewalk book sale that they came across. Cullen had recently decided his new goal in life was to become the gay Bukowski, and while he had started off just stealing the books from the large chain stores, he suspected the employees were starting to catch on and so for the time being was taking a break from crime. Now he was trying to find them used, better cheap than nothing, and was missing only three books: *Factotum, Pulp,* and *Post Office.* He had the rest of the books and all the poetry.

Cullen had taken off fifteen minutes before the rain had begun, with a kiss and a pat on her bum. "Call me tomorrow," he had told her as he walked away, backward so that they could still talk. "I'll probably be back at my place around two. If I'm not, call Griffin and I'll probably still be over at his apartment."

"Okay," she agreed. He was about to bump into someone, a suit on a cell phone who was staring at the ground and not paying any attention to his surroundings. She pointed. "Turn around, Cullen, or change course."

"Call me." And with that, he turned *and* changed course, just narrowly missing the ever-oblivious suit.

"Tell Griffin 'hi' for me," she called and he raised and waved his hand to acknowledge what she'd said.

She walked past cafes and apartment buildings and corner groceries, watching people as she passed and trying to guess which of them were tourists. Usually the tourists had slightly widened eyes and parted lips, taking in everything like they had stumbled into some magic place. She couldn't understand that what was so magical about endless cement and POST NO BILLS signs and crowded streets smelling of garbage and hot dogs.

She wasn't entirely sure of where she was going, but it wasn't home. Home was too empty, a three-room apartment in Queens that she shared with her mom, who worked nights and slept days, and her never-there older sister whose artist boyfriend had a fashionable, expensive loft in Soho with chrome walls and barely any furniture. So she continued moving along the sidewalk, crossing streets when she felt like it, not caring about where she would ultimately end up.

Until the rain.

Becca stood by the gates trying to come up with somewhere she could go. She watched people moving back and forth, in and out, in various states of wetness, going about their lives.

"Can you move?"

An older woman stood behind Becca, wanting specifically to be able to walk where Becca was standing, despite the space all around the girl's not-particularly-large form.

But she couldn't think of the words required to respond rudely, so instead she pulled her MetroCard from her pocket and stepped forward, swiping it automatically and then stepping through. Once on the other side, she hesitated a moment, and in that time the woman paused beside her and, scowling, said, "You shouldn't stand in the way."

"I didn't mean to," stumbled from her mouth.

"Jesus knows what you mean to do." The lady's eyes bore into her own. Maybe the woman didn't even care about where Becca'd been standing, maybe the woman could see through to who she was and just wanted to opportunity to put her down.

She thought of saying, *Seriously? Well, could you—next time you guys are shooting the shit or whatever—could you ask him to give me a call and let* me *know what I mean to do? Cause I'm at a loss.* She thought of giving the old lady the finger. About a million lightning-quick scenarios flashed through her mind, all of which ended with Becca feeling like a rock star and this old woman looking offended and being without words. Instead, the woman got tired of Becca's blank stare and walked past her without a look back.

The subway was cold and it seeped through the wet of her clothes. She headed down the steps toward the platform, hoping the woman had disappeared into the crowd and that they wouldn't see each other again. A busker was singing the best version of Elvis Costello's "Alison" that she had ever heard in her life, and she moved toward his voice. He was an angel in a straw hat, his voice making her nostalgic for childhood, for being three years old and lying in a small patch of sunlight on the floor by the window. She pressed her back against the wall and bent down into a sitting position over the dirt-flecked floor. A train came but she didn't move, wanting to hear the end of the man's rendition.

The following song, which she recognized as a cover

of Neil Young's "Only Love Will Break Your Heart," was equally wonderful, but after she had missed three trains listening to him sing she thought that she probably looked ridiculous and decided to get on the next one. As she passed him and moved toward the doors, she wanted to tell him that his music was beautiful. She glanced his way and their eyes met. She broke the gaze, staring ahead. Thankfully the car she'd ended up in was a fairly empty one and she took a corner seat.

Putting her bag on her lap and unzipping it, she rummaged through it to avoid the faces of everyone else on the train. Looking at them made her think, made her wish; filled her head with everything missing in her life. Everything being, in simple summation: Skye Matheson.

Skye had moved to Oregon with her mom six months ago, leaving suddenly without much of a chance for good-bye. There were occasional e-mails— usually of twenty words or less—about how Skye was doing much, *much* better. She'd met another girl, one who forced her to eat, who she actually listened to, who introduced her to loads of music that she was only too happy to suggest to her now ex-girlfriend. Skye and her new, extraperfect girlfriend named Layla. Skye and Layla. How delightful.

People had begun piling onto the train, and with them the murmur of indiscernible voices increased steadily. On the opposite side from where Becca was sitting, an impossibly beautiful girl was leaning against the closed doors. Becca's eyes traveled from the sneakers on her feet up to her black satin loose-fitting pants with a bit of a flare, to the tight T-shirt she was wearing. A tall man dressed in a short red jacket, jeans, and a baseball cap obscured her face, but her bleached blonde hair was visible, clinging together in wavy strands that made it look both messy and styled. Becca wished for the man to move.

He did, at the next stop, and this newfound view allowed Becca to notice how flawless the blonde's skin was, how big and cute her eyes were, how she appeared untouched by the rain. It also allowed her to notice that the girl was not alone, that a baggy-skater-pants-wearing boy was standing right up against her; one arm was behind her head to hold on to the pole, and his other arm reached forward to wind around her waist. Baggy Pants leaned in to kiss the blonde's neck so Becca averted her eyes quickly. Watching couples made her feel sort of like she was an über loser, so drifting alone that she had to watch people clearly in the midst of it just to get her kicks.

Her eyes landed on a girl, sitting one seat to the right of the couple, who also happened to be staring at them. The girl watched for a bit longer before lowering her gaze to her entwined hands, resting in her lap. Becca tilted her head slightly to take in the girl's natural blonde hair: chin length and cutely styled with her bangs short and horizontal across her forehead. She was wearing light blue glasses and her posture looked perfect or else maybe just uncomfortable. Heart-shaped face, button-esque nose. Full, dark red lips contrasted against pale, pale skin.

After another moment, the girl, whom she'd started to think of as "Glasses," raised her eyes again to resume watching the couple. Becca tried to see which person the girl was staring so hard at.

Baggy Pants was holding the blonde's hand now, and they were whispering to each other in that way couples commonly do, his lips right next to her ear and her lips teased up into a smile. They both laughed. She whispered into his ear and they laughed again. Becca was sure that Glasses was focusing on the blonde, though that didn't necessarily mean that she was checking the blonde out; she could just be love lonely and envious of the slightly nauseating scene before them.

She and Skye had been like that once, speaking in whispers and maintaining near-constant physical contact. One afternoon, they had lain in bed and alternated words and kisses for a period of close to six hours. They'd forgotten to eat and had let the machine pick up all calls.

Glasses dropped her eyes again, glancing at all the people around her. She noticed Becca and her expression shifted, looking suddenly startled. Hoping to be reassuring, Becca smiled her nicest, least-frightening-she-hoped smile. It didn't seem to work, because Glasses quickly looked back down at her hands again.

They had reached the next stop and Glasses stood

up and pushed past the few people in her way to get out of the train. Without bothering to zip up her bag, without thinking about what exactly she was doing, Becca jumped up to follow the girl. She walked slowly behind, debating whether or not to actually approach and try to talk to her.

Becca paused, watching, as she headed up the steps. She was in a light blue sweatshirt and black skirt with red rain galoshes and a closed-up umbrella under her arm.

What is wrong with me? Becca thought while at the same time she called out, "Hey!"

Glasses turned around, not actually expecting whoever the voice was to be addressing her. It was the drenched girl. Her brow furrowed and she held out her umbrella like a sword.

"Do I know you?" she asked.

Becca shook her head, which caused Glasses to take a step back, so she quickly added, "But I'm not crazy."

"And the proof of this would be your following of a complete stranger?" With one hand, the other girl adjusted her slightly askew glasses. "Besides, would you really approach me and say 'Why, hello. I am planning to slice you open and eat your heart. Come with me, please.'"

"Do I look like someone who would slice you open and eat your heart?" Becca asked.

Glasses studied her pursuer intensely. Finally: "No." She lowered the umbrella. "Did I drop something?"

"I wanted to know your name, actually." As soon as the words had left her mouth, she couldn't believe them. *Seriously, what is wrong with me?*

"What's *your* name?" Glasses asked, her voice suspicious.

"I'm Becca. I'm from Queens and was taking the subway to avoid going home. So when I saw you take off, you seemed interesting and I thought maybe you might have some time to kill with a procrastinating-going-home stranger."

The girl considered all this for a moment. She passed the umbrella from one hand to another while studying Becca. She held out her hand and said, "Hailey."

Becca shook Hailey's hand and waited for her to continue, watched as she resumed passing the umbrella back and forth.

"What kind of time killing?" Hailey asked.

"Do you actually have time to kill?" Becca asked.

Hailey nodded. "Yes. And an umbrella to defend myself with. I am ready to kick ass, if need be." They began moving up the last of the steps and then Hailey opened her umbrella once they had reached the top. "I'm on my way to a bookstore. St. Mark's."

Another bookshop. "Mind if we stop in at a used clothes shop? I just need something vaguely warm to wear."

Hailey agreed as they huddled under the umbrella, shoulders touching. They were silent for a few blocks before Hailey finally asked, "Why were you watching me?"

"I was watching the couple standing by the doors. I saw you were, too. My mind just went on a run, wondering why you were watching them. I wanted to meet you."

Hailey was surprised for a moment before shaking her head, tightening her expression and looking forward again. Becca's eyes moved to rest on Hailey's small hand wrapped around the umbrella handle. Hailey's nails were painted red and chipping, leaving uniquely formed patterns of polish—tiny, red nail polish clouds.

Hailey led them to forty-three Third Avenue, where they stopped at Metropolis, which both of them had been to before. Hailey seemed to be the proper veteran, even knowing the guy behind the counter by name, and she bantered with him as Becca searched the racks. She'd only been to the shop a few times, and had forgotten how cheap everything was.

Hailey returned to her while she was still shopping, navy blue corduroys held under her arm along with a plain gray T-shirt with a small hole the size of a cigarette burn in the back. She was looking for the final thing she needed, a hoodie. Something warm.

Hailey went to the other side of the rack and began scanning items, occasionally pulling one out to study it. Each time the sweater was returned to its place, though. When Becca had reached the other girl's side, Hailey was holding a hanger in her hand and studying the sweatshirt hanging off of it. It was a black hoodie, not a zip up, with faded orange lettering that spelled OREGON STATE. Her eyes froze on the words in front of her and her heart began to beat too loudly for comfort. "My ex moved to Oregon," she blurted, then felt her eyes widen as she clapped a hand over her mouth. She didn't need to start talking about Skye.

But Hailey turned to her new acquaintance and studied her expression. There was something she couldn't place in the tone. Instead of asking about the ex, she tugged lightly on the pouch of the hoodie, which was slightly unraveled so the corner hung down. "I like this. It makes me feel like someone loved it."

Becca stared at it, chewing the inside of her cheek as she considered the coincidence. Maybe it was a good luck sort of thing. A reminder of badness and goodness at once. She took the sweater without another word, heading up to the cash register.

The employee, a guy with dreads and massively built arms, rang up the items. When Hailey came to join Becca at the counter, he winked at her and then said, "This one is pretty cute."

Becca glanced at Hailey in surprise. This one? This what? Did he assume that they were a couple? Was he giving Hailey his approval on her latest choice in love interests? Did Hailey often come in here with girls— girls who this guy knew she was involved with? Or did he just mean that he thought Becca was cute, totally unrelated to Hailey at all?

Hailey rolled her eyes, giving nothing away. "Don't

be a skeezebot, Derrek. Ring up the damn purchases and maybe I'll come back sometime and continue to give you business."

He laughed, a deep laugh that made him sound pleased by her response. "A skeezebot, she calls me." He repeated it to Becca. "Do you hear that? A skeezebot. Can you imagine how that hurts me?"

He was folding up the cords but Becca clued in and reached for them. "Sorry. I mean, really, really sorry. I want to wear these things since I am going to die of pneumonia if I stay like this."

Without a word, he unfolded the pants and cut off the tag, then cut the tags off the other items too. "Well, it's $48.17," he said and she pulled out her debit card and handed it to him. Sliding it through the machine, he smirked down at the counter in front of him. She pressed all the necessary buttons. Then, as the charge went through, she headed back into the change room and removed her clothes.

"Becca, I got some napkins for you, to dry yourself with."

Becca froze, raising her arms to cover her bra-clad breasts as her mind whirled. Pushing aside the curtain, she poked her head out and Hailey stuffed a stack of napkins into her fist. "You should wipe yourself off as best you can," she suggested and then turned and walked back over to Derrek.

Becca stared after her a moment and then closed the curtain again, dabbing her body with the cheap papers.

She felt less sticky when she put on the new clothes. She walked out of the dressing room and saw Derrek laughing as Hailey did a dance using her umbrella. She held it sideways, a hand on each end, and moved her legs back and forth, side to side. Becca watched, a smile picking up the ends of her lips, but after a moment moved toward the counter.

"Hey," she said, interrupting them. Hailey leaned back immediately against the counter. "Can I have a plastic bag?"

"No problem." Derrek handed her one, smiling in a way she thought seemed sly. He had the sort of eyes one might describe as twinkling. "You girls have a nice day."

"Nice meeting you."

"You too."

It was only drizzling by the time they got outside again, but Becca put her hood over her head as they again huddled beneath the umbrella. "I can't believe how soaked you ended up," Hailey said. "I check the weather before I leave the house everyday."

"That involves a level of organizational skill that I will never have."

Hailey laughed, then asked her randomly, "Where in Queens?"

"Elmhurst." Before Hailey could ask for more detail, Becca cut in with, "What about you? Do you live around here?"

"Yeah, not far."

Once they reached St Mark's, Becca followed Hailey around, still all booked out from earlier. She watched everything Hailey looked at, silently noticing what she picked up and put back: Michelle Tea, George Eliot, James Tate, Ali Smith.

"You aren't looking around," Hailey noticed.

"I was in bookstores all of today. My best friend Cullen wants to be Bukowski and is hardcore researching."

Hailey saw a book just above Becca that caught her eye. She moved forward, almost right up against the other girl, reaching past Becca's head. Their eyes met, and Hailey smiled as she grasped it, ran her hand along the cover. She opened it to the first page and scanned it. Murmuring her approval, she put it back. Suddenly she asked, "Who would you want to be?" She continued looking at the books, but Becca knew that she was waiting for the answer.

"Probably Kelly Link."

"Who?"

"Kelly Link. She writes great modernized fairy tales."

Hailey moved over to the L's and bent down, then reached for *Stranger Things Happen*. She opened it and read the first page of the first story, then closed it and turned back to Becca. "Great first page."

"The cover is like Nancy Drew meets awesome."

Hailey laughed, hugging the book to her chest and heading for the cash register. Once outside, Hailey opened her umbrella again. They stood under it, facing each other. "I have to go," Hailey admitted. "I have a band rehearsal in an hour and I have to do some prerehearsal-y things." Becca nodded as her heart began to pound. *Ask for her number. Just ask.*

All the people moving around her made Becca feel stuck. Boxed in. Could they hear them? Could they see her attempting to ask out the girl next to her? Would they think that was sick?

"I hope you like the book."

"I had a really nice time."

Hailey smiled widely, than looked down at the sidewalk. Becca kept staring at her, trying to force the words from between her lips. When Hailey looked up again and met her awkward gaze, Becca forced herself to smile back. Her glance fixed again on Hailey's clenched hand around the umbrella handle.

"Will I see you again?" Hailey asked, drawing Becca's attention back to her face—her cute heart face and blonde bob and . . . *Just ask. Idiot.*

The rain was lightly thudding against the pavement, making splashing noise in puddles, and it mirrored the sound of her probably-too-loud beating heart.

"I'd like you to," she finally mumbled. *Idiot.*

"So maybe do you want to take my number down?"

Becca scrambled in her bag for her pen and notebook. Pulling both items out, she uncapped the pen, which was then grabbed by Hailey.

Hailey reached out, wrote her name and number on the formerly blank page in front of her. Below that, she wrote, *You have really cute shoulders.* "You going to be okay without my umbrella?" she asked, handing the pen back to Becca.

"I—" Becca was staring. She hadn't realized she could stare at someone so hard. She felt like she was trying to walk along the cracks in the sidewalk, barely balancing. "I—" She shook her head, trying to clear it. "You like my shoulders?"

"I saw them when I handed you the napkins."

"Oh."

Her head felt empty. Her face felt like it was formed into the stupidest of possible expressions—her mouth hanging open like a fish. She forced herself to form and expel words: "I like yours too."

Hailey laughed. "You haven't even seen mine."

"Are we flirting?" Becca managed. "I feel like we might be."

Hailey raised an eyebrow. "Are you going to call me?"

Becca nodded her head. "Very much so. Yes."

"Okay, well. Bye then, mysterious subway girl."

Becca stuffed the pen and notebook back into her bag. "With cute shoulders, apparently."

Hailey moved forward and pressed a kiss to the other girl's material-covered right shoulder. "Exceptionally cute shoulders." She straightened up and pressed her lips to Becca's for an instant, then pulled back. "You mentioned an ex. Is there a current?"

"Oh no. Not since—" she caught herself. *Why would*

you say that? "No," she corrected herself.

"And you don't make a habit of coming onto girls you see on subways?"

"Not usually but this went so well I might start."

"Ha ha," Hailey deadpanned. She reached for the bottom of Becca's hoodie and toyed with it, tugged on it lightly. "Have a good trip home." She let go and pointed at Becca, pressing her finger against the girl's chest. "You call me."

"I will," Becca said and with that Hailey turned away, leaving her standing in the rain and staring. The drops began to hit the top of her head and wet her sweatshirt in small quick darts. She watched Hailey until the girl was completely gone from sight. She watched, the rain fell, and it was nice.

PRELUDES

KATIA NOYES

CYNTHIA WAS HER name, an investment something-or-other who lived next to Gramercy Park. She was small, had striking short black hair that cut across her forehead in a slash, was at least forty (twice Angel's age), and very smart. They met at the airy members' café at MoMA; Angel had a friend who got her in.

When Cynthia spoke from a nearby table and tried to provoke a conversation about the current American landscape exhibit, Angel liked what she had to say and smiled a lot. She wanted to explain how paintings inspired her dancing, and she wanted to talk about Frederic Church's monumental work—but instead she was quiet.

"You have great arms," said Cynthia, as she was leaving.

People often commented on Angel's arms; they were

long and muscular. She splayed them out on the café table, enjoying the feel of having Cynthia look at them, then took Cynthia's card, a card that led to a dinner tonight in Gramercy Park.

Angel had been dating a lot of people since she arrived in New York the previous spring. She had imagined she would only be working, dancing, and performing, but instead she found many of her evenings free. The guy you might call her boyfriend, a cellist, was exquisite, but Angel was only one more girl to him, and a young, unimportant one. He performed at sex, was good at making it sweet. Like Angel, though, what incited him most were thoughts of fame. And like her, he was broke. His skin was smooth as cool marble; he had a perfect nose that flared when he made jokes, but inside he was not quite touchable. He told her stories that had a rehearsed feel. She imagined the other women to whom he had said these things, and it excited her to know she was in a long lineage, that he could sustain his act with as much bravado as he did.

She needed people to think she was special, though, and at times the cellist could do that wonderfully. But. But. He was going to leave her soon, that much she knew. And she thought, "What a narcissist he is!" And then she laughed, because she wondered if maybe she was one, too. It seemed like half of New York had the same diagnosis. At least, she thought, they all shared something.

When she imagined her date tonight, Angel got

nervous. The truth: Angel choked around most people. She felt ditzy. She didn't trust words, or more accurately sentences. A few words here and there were interesting, but once you had to arrange them into sentences they became fascistic. She didn't mind other people talking, but her own words felt overbearing and false. She relied on dance to speak for her, a medium she trusted.

She mainly dated men; they talked easily and her only requirement was to listen. But there had been a few aggressive talky women as well.

A gruff-voiced, long-haired plumber took her to a gay club in Bay Ridge and showed her off, as if they were replaying a scene from a Scorsese movie. She had wanted to bring Angel home, have her Italian mother lecture her about making gravy, give her jewelry bought on Canal Street. Angel yearned to have sex with a really butch woman, but it was clear the courting process was going to take weeks and she had no patience.

There was Liz, the older professor, who brought her back to a place on the Upper East Side. It hadn't been clear what the hell she had wanted Angel to do. House-sit someday? There was some pretense of it anyway. Then Liz said she wanted Angel to be her assistant: "I need you to do massage, water plants, and if you don't have a place to stay, you can sleep here."

There was one bed. "With you?"

"If you would like."

Angel considered it, but the bed was too small. She'd never be able to breathe.

It wasn't clear to her why so many people wanted her around. She had never thought of herself as especially good-looking . . . Well, that wasn't exactly true. She believed she was glamorous and captivating, but until she hit New York, no one else had seemed to notice.

. . . . .

THEY ATE SEA bass with leeks and chanterelles, drank Napa Valley wine—all served by a discreet cook while they sat at a long maple counter. Cynthia, the Gramercy Park investment person, lit up a cigarette and stared at the wall over Angel's head. The large kitchen walls glowed with a burnished blue; the stain-less-steel appliances defied dullness; each object in the room introduced color and shape, from the delicate red Japanese bowls on the open shelves to the large round wall clock. Angel tried to get comfortable on her stool, but the crumbs she had left by the side of her plate made her feel like she was damaging the carefully constructed world.

If Cynthia was trying to seduce her, why did she have the lights turned high? And why was she so stiff? She had the old-time New York mask, the look of someone who had lived on an island forever. Angel had met a few lifelong New Yorkers, and she had learned to recognize the don't-fuck-with-me expression. Apparently even money didn't take it away.

Cynthia was forty? Fifty? Angel couldn't tell her

age. Her olive face, with its fierce expression, was old enough to forfeit pretense. Angel liked a challenge. She appreciated ugly-sexy. As she gazed at Cynthia's imperious nose and dramatic black hair, she thought of the people she had met in the past months who had looked just as unapproachable, as if they didn't know how to stop working long enough to let down their guard.

The intensity of New Yorkers! Angel didn't need to see underneath their masks; the surfaces themselves were enough. And what would it be like to rub up against a woman's body again? To explore. She had done it too few times. So far she had found women mild, not as exciting as men, but you never knew.

"That's why I will see any production in which he does the stage design, even if it's something as tame as *The Pearl Fishers*," concluded Cynthia. Her story was over.

"That's a good thing," said Angel. She hoped it was an appropriate response.

"We could go. It won't be great, but it will be visually arresting."

"I'm game for whatever."

"When you compare Tchaikovsky to early Bizet, though, it's like comparing meat to cream."

Angel nodded.

Cynthia took a sip of her wine, then took a much bigger one, a really long glug, glug. It looked like the way Cynthia would drink if she was alone. It was odd. Maybe she thought of Angel as a stupid, young trick.

Some people did. It didn't bother Angel, but if it was true, she wished they'd get on with it. The thing was, Cynthia didn't seem to care what Angel thought of her. It might be the rich thing. Angel had noticed very rich people often treated others in an absentminded way, as if they were disposable.

"Why don't we leave these and go in the living room," said Cynthia.

When Angel started to carry her plate off the table, Cynthia raised her eyebrows. The cook had served them dinner but then disappeared; Angel thought it would be polite to bus her dish, but when she saw Cynthia's look she put it back down.

An enormous abstract expressionist painting, it must have been an actual Motherwell, covered one wall of the living room. The red and black silhouettes spoke of aggression, blood. Male victory. Angel liked that Cynthia owned it. It dominated the room and made the minimalist furniture look like tiny floating debris on the blue area rug. If the painting spoke of the lesbian side of Cynthia, it said something interesting.

"I feel like dancing," said Angel. She pointed to the Motherwell. "Blame it on that."

Cynthia looked at her like she was crazy. "I see." When she saw Angel was serious she asked, "What do you like to dance to?"

"Chopin. Steve Reich. George Crumb. Ives. Patti Smith. Cuban blues."

Cynthia quietly went over to the glass music cabinet,

which was filled with old record albums. She fingered their long spines and pulled out a tweedy classical something.

Angel took off her shrunken black cardigan. She rolled up her pants and removed her bracelets so that her arms were bare.

Cynthia's place was the largest home she had seen in New York. She wanted to kick back the rug and have the whole wood floor to spin on. Instead she went in the dining room and jogged around the dining room table, which was as big as several pianos.

"Just warming up," she yelled.

The Chopin was hard to resist, but she had to first get her feet going and circulation pumping or she would hurt herself. She ran around the table for a couple minutes and shook her long arms.

Cynthia placed herself on the couch, lit a cigarette, waited for the show.

Angel went into the living room and stood in front of her host, did a few tondus, smiled.

Cynthia nodded. She looked serious, as if she were at a recital. That was good. She took art seriously, even dance. Most people didn't.

"Your house begs to be danced in," said Angel, her voice punctuating the music.

Chopin's piano riffs! Thank God Cynthia had chosen Chopin's *Preludes*, something Angel knew, was introduced to long ago, during her first foray into ballet. Intense living-room music: aristocratic flurries, hot and cold passion, child's playfulness mixed with adult restraint.

Angel walked over to the edge of the room, the side near the hallway, at the lip of the deep-blue rug. She winked at Cynthia. She looked again at the Motherwell painting and then closed her eyes, raised on her toes. The air felt light as she went up. The strangeness of the evening compressed and roped through her until she could shape the impulses into physical translations—an arabesque, a few syrupy glissades, then some jumps, carefully in one place. She laughed at the feel of jumping, always a pleasure to leave the ground. She ran around the dining room table again, did one long kick and a series of pirouettes on the wood floor before walking back to Cynthia, getting down on her knees, and bowing in front of her.

Cynthia blew out a hit of smoke. "My dear. You have talent."

"Thanks."

They were quiet as Angel stretched herself on a long leather chair, put her feet up, and gazed at the high ceiling, finally relaxed.

Cynthia went over to lower the volume. "You're not the right size for ballet, are you?"

Opinions, opinions. New Yorkers thought they knew everything.

"No," said Angel. She was too breasty, a little too much width everywhere, despite her long legs. A classical dancer needed steel straightness, thinness, and length in every inch. She was slim but not tiny; she had very broad shoulders and a head that was a little too large; a neck not quite long enough. She had long ago given up the pink-tights dream. "I'm in dance-theater."

"Well. Let me show you something anyway." Cynthia got up and found a book on a tall bookshelf. She brought it over. It was a biography, one Angel had read, of a Russian ballerina. "My mother gave me this when I was a girl. It was her last gift to me." Cynthia's face changed, became humble and sad. The book was clearly precious, part of a private history.

Angel took the book and opened it slowly. She spent some time looking, as if she hadn't read it before, all the while disturbed to have seen Cynthia get soft, to see her stiff expression fall, her eyes get watery. Vulnerability made everyone alike: You could paint one portrait of the human soul with the same title, "Help me!" It sickened Angel, and for some reason, made her want to run. She knew the feeling of sorrow overtaking Cynthia, but did not want to allow it safe harbor.

Cynthia straightened her posture and began to speak about ballet, the relationship between the Russian Revolution and innovation. Modernity.

"Well, it's getting late," concluded Cynthia, perhaps fearing that she had lost Angel's interest.

"Yes, I better get going."

"I'll help get you a cab."

No way could she afford a cab home. "No, that's fine."

"Thank you for dancing. You are—"

Cynthia stopped. For the first time that evening she didn't finish a sentence. She coughed and stood up.

Angel began muttering. "Thanks for watching. For giving me an incredible dinner."

It was clear they would never see each other again. And that being so, they looked at each other. Eye to eye. The intimacy of an ending.

To open any further, one of them would have to crack.

As they said good night, Angel wondered if she was scared. Did the thought of making love to a woman as old and smart and rich as Cynthia overpower her?

No. It didn't. It wasn't the sex that scared her. She wished sex could scare her. This wasn't about sex. It was something else.

"Let me see you out," said Cynthia.

As she stood by the door, Cynthia spoke to her for the last time. "You are a beautiful girl." At that moment Angel smelled the wine on Cynthia's breath; they were standing quite close. She realized Cynthia was drunk. Or high. Or both. A pool of lust appeared in Cynthia's eyes.

Angel reached out to take Cynthia's hand. Cynthia looked baffled.

Angel bent down and kissed it. Her hand smelled like tobacco, but not just that. Lime, salt, blood . . . ? Her flesh smelled of something poetic and hidden, something Angel wanted to find, was curious about, yet never could identify.

"Good night," said Angel, running down the marble stairs. At the sidewalk, she looked back over her shoulder to wave but the door had already closed. Disoriented, Angel forgot which way led back to the subway. She made a blind guess and forged ahead.

LAGUARDIA

RUTHANN ROBSON

COMING HOME.

There, she said it. Not out loud, thankfully, although traveling alone could cause disorienting blurts from anyone. Even people who did not prize articulation as much as she did might be found murmuring to themselves or starting conversations with others in certain circumstances. Despite her occupation and interests—some might even say obsessions—she was not one of those people who reached out with agreeable phrases simply because she found herself in someone's proximity. She was self-possessed and stealthy, traits set in some low-life, low-lying swamp, even before she had flown into LaGuardia for the first time, twenty-six years ago.

That's why it was odd, then and even now whenever she thought of it, which was almost every day, that she had not only smiled at Lucia in the airport baggage claim but had whispered something like "hey." Her smile was only for a fraction of a fraction of a second; she was sure of that. And her whisper was no ordinary twenty decibel whisper, she was sure of that too. She'd bet it had been below the normal threshold of hearing.

"Need a ride?" Lucia had asked.

Shit, Jayne had thought to herself. These New York City women were forward. She was not even here an hour—and hadn't even gotten to her first women's bar—and she was already being picked up. And by a woman who could certainly be labeled a "looker." Tall, and made taller by the heeled boots which clung tightly to her calves; what the folks back home would call "big-boned." Lucia had big breasts, a big solid ass, big hair that was not teased but long and voluminous, curly, big lips, huge eyes, and mammoth silver hoop earrings.

It was the voice, however, that impressed Jayne. Lucias had a lax voice, with a long slow rise to it, so that her words seemed both suspenseful and inevitable. The pitch of the consonant "*d*" was only slightly higher than the vowels, a rarity that resulted in a smooth pattern. The tone radiated warmth and welcome.

Still, Jayne was shy. And maybe even a tiny bit wary. What kind of woman hangs around the airport looking for dates? Though perhaps—surely!—she was here for another reason. Yes, she was probably picking up someone else. Jayne looked around hopefully for a matched set of elderly parents, wizened and doting, not as tall as Lucia but bearing their resemblance to their daughter in a regal manner. Jayne had been told not to believe the rumors that New York City was unfriendly—"don't be afraid to ask for directions if you need them; people will be glad to help you"—and this must be the proof. She hadn't even had to ask.

The wariness dispelled for the moment, Jayne's shyness increased. If she had to speak again, Jayne knew that this woman would be able to instantly plumb the depths of Jayne's failings. First there was Jayne's accent. Of course, Jayne knew Lucia had an accent. Hell, everyone had an accent. But some accents were sexier than others. Jayne's own Florida accent was clearly not among the attractive ones, even if Jayne had an expert elocution perfected during her years of schooling. She was here for even more schooling.

"You'll be able to do anything you damn well please," one of her pals had said to her before she left, "after you get that fancy New York degree." Jayne had not argued.

But people in New York City—this woman right here—would know that there was nothing fancy in her immediate future. Jayne was going to Queens College, not far from this very airport. She'd been thrilled when she was accepted into the graduate speech pathology program, but then certain details—like location—had seemed less promising.

She gathered courage from small signs, including her travel agent. She had been talking to the travel agent about what airport to fly into for her first trip to New York, and the travel agent had asked where the school was and where she would be living. When Jayne had admitted Queens, the travel agent had exclaimed she was "so very, very lucky" since "both of the airports were right there." The lift in the travel agent's voice had almost been enough to convince Jayne that there wouldn't be 160-decibel jet takeoffs assaulting her hearing every day.

LaGuardia had the cheaper flights. Also it sounded more exotic. JFK, the other airport, sounded overly familiar. There were schools in Florida named for the dead president, though he had not been popular there while he was alive. But what or who was LaGuardia?

So, here she was, at the airport that was in fact named for someone, a long ago mayor of the city, as she'd learned. It would have been nice, Jayne thought, if the airport had been named "Little Flower," that mayor's nickname, though perhaps that sounded too treacly for such an important city? A bit of flowery perfume would also have been welcome. At the luggage claim, the woman pressed against her, smelling of sweat. She was so close that she was able to grab the suitcase as Jayne's fingers were about to brush its handle.

Too aggressive, Jayne had thought then. The slow voice that promised languid and luxurious romance was contradicted by such an assertive gesture.

Jayne had turned, pulling the suitcase away from Lucia's grasp.

"C'mon," Lucia had said. Her voice was pitched higher, pleading almost, and unattractively girlish.

"I don't think so," Jayne had answered.

"Cheap for you. For real." Lucia's tone vibrated along the lower registers.

Double shit, Jayne had thought to herself. This woman was a—a hooker. Jayne recoiled. She had been in New York City how long? Not even out of the airport and she had already seen the ugly underbelly of urban life. Lesbian prostitutes. She wasn't even going to wonder how this woman had identified her as a dyke. Maybe it was better that she wasn't going to Manhattan, that she'd be living in some basement apartment near Queens College, at an address which seemed to be nothing but numbers.

"I don't have any money," Jayne lied.

"Well, then, how you gonna get where you're going? I don't see anyone picking you up?"

"I'll be taking a taxi, thank you," Jayne replied, despite the fact that she thought she should not say another word to this woman.

"Of course. Exactamente. And that is me. Lucia. Your taxi."

Gypsy cab. The phrase came to Jayne from some guidebook she had read, or maybe the travel agent had mentioned it. But what she knew was that it was something to be avoided. Disreputable. Dangerous. One should always choose yellow and a medallion.

"No thank you," Jayne said. It was impossible that

Queens College had sent someone to pick her up, wasn't it? Had she even told anyone she'd be arriving at LaGuardia?

Jayne strode outside the terminal. She saw the line of well-dressed travelers and joined the queue. She heard the harsh whistle of the man who seemed to be the traffic director and cab procurer. Did she have to tip him?

As the line moved, she watched with relief as no one else seemed to be handing him anything. She reached the front of the line sooner than she had estimated, the cabs whizzing around despite what seemed to Jayne to be unmoving traffic, and she hefted her suitcase into the trunk which had magically opened.

Jayne recited the string of numbers of her new address to the cabdriver. He shook his head.

She repeated the numbers. She knew she had them right, but perhaps his English comprehension was not sufficient. Was everyone here from someplace else?

He shook his head again, and as Jayne started to state the numbers again, more clearly and more slowly, he was at the trunk and heaving her suitcase onto the pavement.

"Queens? Queens! No Queens," he had shouted, and then argued with the man with the whistle. The cab zoomed off, empty. Jayne turned to the man with the whistle for assistance, who shrugged, and motioned her to go to the end of the long line.

Jayne had felt humiliated. There was no other word

for it. Humiliated.

She had not been able to speak. Aphasia: the loss of language. The definition was one Jayne had studied, but had never experienced. A more seasoned New Yorker—Jayne, now—would have taken down the medallion number, demanded a new cab and driver from the cab director, and would have filed a complaint with the Taxi and Limousine Commission. But this new-to-New York Jayne turned and went back inside the terminal, more to escape anyone who had witnessed her abasement than to implement alternative plan. She had no fall back.

Lucia had been there, leaning on a wall, looking toward the escalator that might bring her a passenger.

"How much to Queens College?" Jayne had asked. She kept her tone as even as she could.

"Ah, girl. I live right near there. And not much happening here. I take you home—ten dollars."

"Deal," Jayne had said.

The transaction was more difficult to consummate than either Jayne or Lucia had expected, since they had trouble finding the apartment. They had started talking, Jayne sitting in the front seat of Lucia's black sedan, confessing it was her first time in New York, Lucia offering the fact that she had not been in the city, or in the country, very long herself. When she had memorized the address, Jayne had concentrated on the numbers but had neglected the designations of street/avenue/place/terrace, never imagining that 172nd

Street would not be followed by 173rd Street, but by 172nd Terrace, and then 172nd Place, and then 172nd Avenue. Lucia, for her part, was not as familiar with the area and did not live as close by as she had implied. Jayne had wanted to give Lucia twice what they had agreed, but Lucia wanted to take half as much. In the end, they agreed on the ten dollars and Lucia took Jayne's number, that is, the telephone number for the graduate program where Jayne would be a student.

Jayne had a message on her first day as a graduate student.

"A call for you," the secretary, who was also a graduate student, had said as soon as Jayne had introduced herself. "A clear tone, slight stammer. A Spanish syntax, probably Central rather than South American? But very nice enunciation."

Welcome to the Speech Department, Jayne had thought. She did not need to look at the pink "While You Were Out" slip to know the call had been from Lucia. Although she had not detected a stammer when they had spoken in person. Lucia must have been anxious on the phone.

During her first class, introduction to speech pathology, Jayne listened to the professor lecture about the professionalization processes and history of "speech correction" and the gaps between "theory and therapy." The professor had a precisely modulated voice, which sounded overly practiced and thus somewhat insincere to Jayne. None of the students asked questions, even when invited, which seemed to Jayne quite understandable.

Jayne learned about narrative construction in children, which did not seem to her to be related to how a speech therapist might help a child correct a lisp, but was obviously a subject of some passion among some of the professors. There were those who believed in the "whole language" approach and those who favored training in specific psycholinguistic skills. Jayne, like most of the other students, found the discussions rather abstract, if not arcane.

· · · · ·

ON THE PLANE circling over LaGuardia Airport now, almost two and a half decades later, Jayne was no more dedicated to one theory of narrative production than she had been as a student. She believed stories shifted and pulsed with time and purpose. The notion of an "abnormal story"—a story without a resolution, for example—remained an uncomfortable assessment. One of her professors had called her "episodic," Jayne recalled. She had told Lucia about it, who had thought it had sounded like a wonderful compliment. "Adventuresome," Lucia had whispered, throaty and breathy, in that particular way that Jayne had started to crave.

Lucia had also said "Your breasts are blue." Jayne remembered this precisely, vividly, exactamente. It was the first time they had been naked together. They were in Jayne's apartment and the moonlight—or street-light—seeped into the bedroom. At first, Jayne did not comprehend. She was still dizzy with all the other words Lucia had been saying, which sometimes formed themselves into sentences, and sometimes not. It was a fantasy that Jayne had not even known she had had: a lover whose voice caressed as artfully as her hands did. Lucia did not instruct, or coax, or make baby noises. Instead, her words cascaded like hair, permeating the air like the smell of a subtle perfume, resonating with a rhythm that seemed to originate inside Jayne.

"Azul." Lucia was laughing now.

Jayne thought that maybe some of the dye from her shirt had colored her skin. Certainly she had been sweating enough. And she was not fond of undergar-ments, at least on her own body.

Then she realized her shirt, now on the floor, was yellow.

She looked down at her own breasts, iridescent against the rest of her body which had been tanned by the Florida sun. She did not tend to go topless. So Lucia obviously meant Jayne's veins, visible through her cloud-white skin, pulsing blue in the night.

"Blame my ancestors," Jayne said flatly.

"Ah, I do. But let me be your sun. I will tan you all over. Warm you. Golden you."

Jayne thought that sounded suspect. Racist, really. But also sexy. Although almost anything Lucia said seemed sexy to Jayne.

It wasn't long before Jayne and Lucia were living together in an apartment on 161st Terrace. Jayne's basement hovel had been flooded in the first hard rain and Lucia wanted to move away from some noisy neighbors with a large dog. Or so Lucia had said.

Jayne had said "Manhattan."

"Do you know how expensive that is?" Lucia had asked. "Besides, we are close to LaGuardia and JFK airports here. To my work. And to your school. Maybe when you finish? Maybe then, we'll move."

Queens seemed like a lie to Jayne. Forest Hills, Fresh Meadows, Kew Gardens. But no hills or meadows or gardens. No forest, no freshness, and what was a kew? Utopia? What a joke. Jamaica? Get real! It was a borough of fake Tudor and real slums.

In the grit and grime of Manhattan—the city!—one could hum "I live on the Upper / Lower / Eastside / Westside / Chelsea / Village/ Soho." To say "Jackson Heights, Queens" had no heft, no caché, and no history. In Hells Kitchen, Jayne imagined, the putrid smell of summer would be more romantic and the freezing sting of winter would be more dramatic. The car alarms would be a distant dream. The clunk, clunk of the elevator when they made love would not be a problem; they would have a walk-up. Although, Jayne had to admit, the stuttering elevator was obscured by Lucia's soothing voice as she stroked Jayne's pulsing breasts.

Body to body, night after night, Jayne and Lucia

invented a language and practiced elocutions and orations. Inhaling her exhale, sucking her sounds, and wiping Lucia's sweat from her body, Jayne felt that she did not live in Queens, or New York, or any country in the world.

The apartment in winter was so hot that Jayne felt she suffered from a fever in a tropical clime.

"We should not have rented the top floor," she complained.

"We didn't. This is only the fifth floor. Buildings in Queens mostly have six floors."

"Open the window," Jayne said. She still did not understand how an apartment could not be entitled to a thermostat. The superintendent had murmured something about the radiator, but it had no dial, and could not be touched without inflicting blistering burns.

The apartment in summer was no better. A hotbox, Jayne thought, a form of torture that had been used in some war or other. The wars were in another part of the world these days, and she tried not to speak of them, although she found herself shouting at the radio some days, as if she were crazy. Air conditioners blew the fuses.

Despite the heat, they made love. As intensely, if not as often, as the months and then the years whispered along, hushing their predecessors with the vocabulary of the new.

Jayne would worry, now and then, whether they had enough sex. It seemed to her, in the conversations she had and the articles she read, that frequency was important. Sometimes she felt as if it were a matter of hygiene, something like brushing one's teeth, not to be enjoyed but to be tallied. It was the way of Manhattan, she thought.

In Queens, there were dreamy evenings that started in the late afternoon and lasted until the early morning. They might have been to lunch nearby, at some ethnic eatery that had not been mentioned by any food critic, only one of their friends. They tried Greek and Chinese and Indonesian and Peruvian and Irish and Mongolian and Czech and Azerbaijani and even Italian and Thai. They favored places where the food was authentic and fresh and untranslatable. Jayne would smile when there was no menu. Lucia liked to describe the food as she ate it, to speculate about flavors and aromas. Usually, they would go back to their respective days, but sometimes they went to their apartment.

Their apartment, where the sounds of the flights from LaGuardia could be heard whenever the windows were open. Despite the noise, they stayed in the same apartment even after Jayne graduated and was employed by Elmhurst Hospital Center as a speech therapist for stroke victims. Soon, Lucia left the romance of a gypsy cabdriver for the prestige of a translator at a battered women's shelter.

They did meet friends in Manhattan, usually for dinner, sometimes for some experimental performance they pretended to enjoy.

"You have been together so long," one or the other friend would say, her tone tinged with both admiration and disdain.

"Must be that Queens lifestyle," one of them teased, though she herself had been living with her ex-lover for the past seven years, sleeping on the couch of the Chelsea apartment that bound them.

"It must be difficult for her to have sex," Jayne had said to Lucia on the E train back to Queens.

Lucia had laughed. "We could tell her about the subway. Or the airport, even."

Jayne had not planned on booking the next available flight from LaGuardia. Her brother's stroke was premature and unexpected. She had not been there—home—for twenty years.

So much had changed. She used the Internet rather than a travel agent; she had to remove her shoes and her belt and her jacket at the security checkpoint. As the flight descended, she could see the water, looking tropically aqua, but the flat green of her childhood had been conquered by peach stucco. Driving from the airport, she could feel that it was still warm and fetid, warmer it seemed, but it looked more like Queens than she would have imagined. The condos were smashed together like apartment buildings. And the traffic!

Her brother Jude was similar to the other stroke victims she had known, wanting desperately to talk and becoming frustrated, then angry. But she judged his condition better than she had feared. Lucia told her she could hear the relief in her voice when they spoke on the phone that first evening.

Jayne intervened with this nurse and that doctor, taking charge of his medical care. Every patient needs an advocate, Jayne had learned. More so if the patient cannot talk. Soon, Jude was at a rehabilitation center, speaking competently if not expertly. The staff adored him. Especially a certain nurse, who also seemed to respond to Jayne.

"You are so brave to be out," the nurse said to Jayne.

Jayne shrugged. She had not recalled discussing her sexuality.

"Just don't think everyone can be as brave as you are. This is a different place, after all. This is not New York, where you're from."

Jayne shrugged again. Should she admit she was not from New York City, but from the borough of Queens? Or that she was not "from" any part of New York, but had been born nearby, before the word condominium had been invented? Or should she struggle for one of the other replies that were occurring to her, each of which seemed to feature the number "six"? Did you hear it was 2006? Do you know I've been "out" since I was sixteen? Do you think that being a dyke is six six six, the mark of the beast?

Sometimes it is most difficult not to speak.

She did not mention the nurse to Lucia. Even when the nurse was nice enough to give Jayne a ride home— home being a hotel efficiency—when Jayne's rental car would not start. One step led to another, until the nurse was sitting on the green couch and they were talking about ordering dinner. Jayne could almost taste a certain Bangladeshi spice she liked, but pizza was as flavorful as could be managed. Jayne did not say that the slice tasted like cardboard with catsup.

The nurse was tan, Jayne noticed. There was a certain frisson, a tension, some possibility. And who would know?

Despite the rationalizations, it was Jayne's body that was most loyal to Lucia. Even as Jayne wondered if the nurse's skin would be smooth, if her tan line would cut low to her nipples, her hand refused to reach. She could not imagine this woman's nasal voice mumbling in her ear. Or this woman's narrowed eyes looking at Jayne's own white breasts.

When Jude was ready to be discharged into the care of their younger sister, newly divorced, Jayne was relieved for more than the obvious reasons.

The plane tilted toward LaGuardia, circling and circling. "Traffic," the pilot announced. The water below looked brilliantly blue, shimmering in the distance. Excitement rose in her throat. Her ears popped from the change in altitude.

A blast of cold air when she stepped off the plane felt welcoming, as did the sight of Lucia, after Jayne had tromped through the long corridor toward the baggage claim. Lucia's hair was not as long or her earrings as large, but her boots still clung as tightly to her calves as they had all those years ago.

"Need a ride?" Lucia whispered in Jayne's ear, holding her close. Lucia's voice had lost none of its lax rhythm, the long slow rise of it as seductive as ever.

Jayne felt her slacks dampen.

"I'll be taking a taxi," Jayne replied. She tried to sound serious, but her voice echoed giddily in her own ears.

"Ah, a taxi. What if I tell you that I am your taxi? Sent by your lover to get you home as soon as possible so that she might inspect your breasts, to see if they still have an articulate luminosity."

In their hot apartment, the open windows sucked in the sounds of the airplanes from LaGuardia, the car alarms and horns, and some sort of argument in a language neither of them understood. They had walked to Nick's Pizza, and then back through the brick buildings, sleet stinging their faces as they laughed and held hands. Now Jayne could taste the garlic on Lucia's lips, her tongue, and even, it seemed, her neck.

"Your breasts. They are still blue," Lucia said.

"I've missed my sun," Jayne stammered.

Lucia's phrases caressed Jayne, whose slacks would have been drenched had she still been wearing them. In the far distance, she could hear the clunk, clunk of the elevator.

Coming home, Jayne said. Perhaps out loud. Very loud.

PAST IMPERFECT

GENEVA KING

MY GRADUATION DAY should be the happiest day of my life. It's clearly my mother's. She's been singing all morning that her baby is finally going to be able to support her for a change.

"I'm so proud of you." She hugs me for the millionth time, then picks at my robes. "I'm going before your Dad gives away my seat."

"Okay." I'm not paying much attention to her. Heather and her family are standing a few feet away from us, and her mother is fixing her hair. Heather looks my way, but I turn away like I didn't see her.

My mom doesn't miss a thing. "Still not talking to her?"

"Let's not talk about that." I need to concentrate on not tripping over the stage, not on my ex.

"Have it your way. Make sure you wave to me."

As she leaves, I see Heather start walking toward me. I'm not in the mood, so I take off for the nearest bathroom. Luckily, the stalls are empty, so I slide into one and lock it before she comes in.

. . . . .

HEATHER HAD BEEN my best friend since I started at NYU. She was cute, in an artsy dork kind of way. We met early one morning in the bathroom, both of us griping about our insanely early class. We became inseparable after that.

Junior year, she invited me to come home with her over spring break. Since it was cheaper to get to Brooklyn than to DC, I gratefully accepted.

I loved her parents, even though their religious devotion startled me. My mom had been a big fan of sleeping in on Sundays, so spiritual guidance had been sparse, when she chose to give it. Nevertheless, Heather's parents embraced their daughter's heathen friend with open arms.

"You both are way too thin." Mrs. Rubin clucked her tongue as she surveyed us. "Go get settled and we'll have lunch."

I know for a fact that Heather and I were struggling to fit into our fat jeans, but we weren't about to argue with someone who thought otherwise. Especially when that person was baking pies from scratch.

Since her family was having the guest room redone,

we both slept in Heather's room. It was small, but the double bed could easily accommodate both of us. And when we snuggled under the covers that night, Mrs. Rubin came to tuck us in.

"You two all right in there? Need any more blankets?"

"No, ma'am."

"Did you say your prayers?" Mrs. Rubin crossed the room and pulled the covers around our necks.

"Yes, ma'am."

"Sweet dreams." She kissed our foreheads then left, closing the door behind her.

I lay there for a while, listening to the rain fall on the roof. I thought Heather had fallen asleep until she nudged me.

"You awake?"

"Yeah. What's up?"

"I want to ask you something."

She didn't continue, so I tried to help her. "About?"

"You can't laugh at me."

"I won't."

"Or make fun of me."

I sat up and turned to face her. "Heather, what's going on?"

"Okay, so you remember the party?"

I remembered it. Every year, the Rainbow Alliance hosted a party to promote safe sex toy use. My roommate had enjoyed the night. A small cover charge got us a goodie bag with condoms, lube, and a cheap but effective vibrator. Heather, whose upbringing hadn't included such things, had blushed through the entire evening. Unlike a lot of girls in our dorm, we were both virgins; her for religious reasons, and me because I hadn't met Ms. Right yet.

"What about it?"

Another long pause. This time I didn't try to rush her. She'd spill when she was ready. In the meantime, I lay back down and got comfy.

"So I tried it."

"And?" I tried not to laugh. I had promised.

"It didn't work." She shifted, so I could only see her ear in the light. "I tried three times with and without the toy."

I searched for the right words. "It takes a while. You'll learn, I promise." I patted her arm. "When I first started, it took two hours, no lie."

She mulled it over. "Fair enough. So, my question. What do you do?"

"To get off? I don't know." I frowned, trying to remember if there was a certain combination of movement that sent me over the edge. "I mean, I just play with it. Circle it, rub it; sooner or later something's bound to work." Absentmindedly, I started touching myself through my panties.

"It's too much friction," she said a moment later.

I hadn't realized she'd been practicing right next to me. "You have to wet it."

"With what?"

Heather was driving me nuts with her questions, especially since my work was paying off. "Saliva's good. Your own juices."

I heard her sharp intake of breath. "Gross. Forget it. I'm done."

I giggled. "Use some lube then." I know I should have stopped; after all, I was a guest in her bed. But I felt myself getting closer to my peak, so I kept on until I felt a familiar warmth spread through my body.

"Did you just have an . . . an orgasm?"

I couldn't tell from her voice whether she was angry or not, so I stuck with honesty. "Yeah."

Silence. Then, "Show me."

"You want to watch me do it?" If Heather couldn't handle juice talk, how was she going to be able to look at a pussy without flinching? Besides, I wasn't sure how I felt about putting on such an intimate performance.

"No, like—" She stuttered something awful when she got flustered. Now, she could barely get the words out. "Just show me."

When I look back on that night, I still have no clue how we reached that moment. I'd known girls who experimented with kissing each other, maybe a little light touching, but nothing like what was happening now. I don't know if my hesitation stemmed more from shock or the need to protect myself from her.

I heard her get up and root around in her bag. When she climbed back in bed, I reached for her and pulled her against my body, so that her buttocks nestled against my damp panties. My left arm caressed her breast, while my other grasped her palm.

"Squirt some on our hands. Use as much as you want."

As the sticky liquid cascaded over my fingers, I became aware of my heart thudding against her back. She was as nervous as I; her breathing came in short bursts. Her shoulder rested just below my mouth and I resisted the urge to kiss the smooth skin. Instead, I lowered our hands until I found her clit.

"Tell me when it feels good."

She nodded. I kept my middle finger below hers so she could feel the patterns I was making. Her pussy felt familiar, but weird and different from my own. The whole time I tried to keep playing with her nipple.

She moaned, arching into me. I forced myself to remember what this was, to stop wanting to taste her body instead of just touch it.

"Wait, stop." She pulled my hand away.

"What's the matter?"

She sounded frantic. "It's too much . . . the feeling . . . we've got to stop."

I did kiss her shoulder then, to reassure her. "It's okay. Trust me." I replaced my hand and continued stroking her.

Heather whimpered. I took my hand from her breast and covered her mouth. "Go ahead. It's okay."

She was close. She took control of my hand, rocking her cunt against it in a desperate attempt to gain her release. I held her as she shuddered and cried out, sinking against me for support.

We lay curled up for a while. Her breathing returned to normal. I waited for the inevitable recoil as she came back to her senses. To my surprise, she turned toward me and started running her fingers over my face. She traced my cheekbones, nose, and lips. Then she pulled herself up and kissed my lips.

When I think back to that night, the kiss surprised me the most. Something so sweet and personal; and despite all my attempts, I lost a bit of my heart to her then and there. So the next morning, when she wouldn't look me in the eye, it hurt, even though I had been expecting it.

"This—all this—is a major sin. It can't happen again. God will never forgive us." She looked scared at the thought of eternal damnation. "I mean, I know you—and I'd never, but—" She broke off, embarrassed. "You're still my best friend."

"Now you know how to do it yourself, you don't need my help." I made the joke to shut her up; I didn't want to think about the mess anymore.

To my great surprise, our friendship didn't end after that trip. We still hung out back at school, although I noticed she made a point of never being alone with me. It was like we had just decided not to ever mention it again, which was fine with me. If someone had asked whether I was in love with her at that point, I could have honestly said no. Maybe I was on some level, I don't know, but I avoided thinking about her in any romantic light, so I wouldn't tempt myself to develop nonplatonic feelings for her.

Life continued like that until the end of the spring term. Most of the residents, including my roommate, had left for home. Heather and I remained with a few others because we had the misfortune of a Saturday final.

That night, while I dried off after a shower, someone knocked on my door. I opened it to find Heather, looking at me in my towel. I thought she was ready to bolt.

"I'm sorry for what I said."

I frowned. "Are you talking about the Hemingway debate? Heather, I couldn't care less about that."

"No, no, no." She lowered her voice. "The thing. At my house."

"Oh. Don't worry about that either."

"Can I come in? Thanks."

She pushed past me into my room. I sighed, then closed the door. I purposely stayed by the closet and searched for my hairdryer.

She paced a short line back and forth. "I'm so sorry."

"Heather, please. It's fine." I turned on the dryer to drown her out. "I knew how you felt before. We just . . . got caught up. No big."

She glared at me, then stormed over and grabbed the dryer from my hand. "Would you listen to me?"

"I really don't want to go down this road with you. And I need to finish—"

"I love you."

I wondered if excessive heat could addle your hearing.

The dryer fell from her hand. "I do. I love you and I really tried not to cuz it's so wrong, it's so wrong." She kissed me. "If my family knew, they'd kill me, but I don't care cuz I love you." She grabbed my shoulders and kept kissing me between declarations.

I stepped backward. Heather scared me; her eyes were bright and shiny with some emotion I couldn't pinpoint. A part of me soared to hear her finally acknowledge what had happened and utter the words I'd longed for her to say. But a bigger part couldn't shake the feeling that it was just a setup for an even larger fall.

She took a deep breath and touched my face. "I mean it, Gena. I want to be with you."

"But?"

She shifted. "Can we keep it secret for a bit? At least for the summer. So we can get a chance to sort things out for ourselves first."

There wasn't anything for me to sort out by that point in time. I wanted her more than I'd let myself admit. As for my mom, she claimed she'd known I was a lesbian since I was in second grade. I had nothing to hide from her. But Heather's family wasn't my own, and I'd had longer to deal with these feelings than she had.

"Okay."

She grinned. "Okay?"

I laughed with her. "Yeah, okay. Come here." I kissed her, needing to taste her mouth again.

We spent the rest of that night kissing and watching TV, although later I couldn't remember a single show we saw. There seemed to be a silent agreement that we wouldn't go much further. After all, with the exception of the night at her parents', we were both still untouched. More importantly, I think we both recognized the need to take things slow, even though I got wet whenever we were together.

To stay together, we found jobs in the city and an apartment to share a couple of weeks later. Our parents thought it was the perfect arrangement. Two almost-adults learning the way of the world, while at the same time protecting each other from the big city.

The apartment wasn't much, a small two-bedroom with old furniture, but it was ours. Granted, the other room was mostly for show, as we slept in the same bed each night, nuzzling under the sheets. Soon, we upped the ante. Our fondling became more explorative as we sought out new ways to make each other come.

As the summer went by, her family remained clue-less about her new lifestyle. At first it was fun, coming up with lies about the men we were dating.

"He took me to a jazz concert last night. But I don't think I'm gonna keep him. He had really bad breath." She winked at me. "Yes, Ma, Gena has a date tomorrow,

I think. He's a museum attendant." She rolled her eyes. "Dear lord, she's still a virgin. We both are."

That gave us a good laugh, but we both felt the strain from lying. I didn't push her; it was something she had to do in her own time, but it still hurt that I couldn't fully claim her as mine, couldn't be given a chance to be accepted by her parents.

Then, in August, I took her down to the Central Park Zoo to celebrate our last night of freedom. It was the happiest I remember being. Heather and I held hands all afternoon, sometimes ducking behind exhibits to kiss. It was one of those days that made you think that everything is going to be perfect from then on, when nothing could be further from the truth.

"What are we doing now?"

I brushed a leaf out of her hair. "Monkeys?"

She shook her head. "They creep me out. I want to see the polar bears. Oh, they have penguins too!"

"Excuse me, ladies."

We turned to find a man standing behind us, a grave expression on his face.

I clutched Heather's waist. "May we help you?" I'd inherited my mother's attitude. The stranger must have sensed it because he stared coldly at me.

"Have you thought about the state of your souls?"

Oh great, just what I freaking needed. "Come on." I pulled Heather away, but the man blocked our path.

He spoke just to her. "Jesus loves you. His is the only path to take." He gestured to our entwined hands, looking disgusted. "This is not natural. It'll lead you straight to hell!"

"Move it or I'm screaming for the cops!" I looked at Heather. She stood still, her eyes fixed on the man.

"Anytime you want to choose eternal life, come find me. I'm Father Jacob from the church on 72nd Street. Come to Jesus before it's too late." He glared at me one last time and turned to leave.

"God, I can't believe those fucking people. Are you okay?" Heather's face was too pale for my comfort. I decided she needed some food. We walked toward the cafeteria and looked at some animals, but the joy had been zapped from the outing.

"He's right, you know. Us, this, it's wrong." Her eyes sought mine. "No matter how good it feels, it'll never be right."

"Not this shit again." I broke away from her. "I love you. You know that. But I can't go through this up and down with you all the fucking time. Yes, people think it's wrong; people will always look down on us. So what?"

"You don't understand. You have to believe in God to get it."

That stung. "Well, if this is the kind of man he is, I don't want him anywhere in my life."

We stood there for what seemed like eternity. My arms were folded over my chest and she examined the dirt. The unease I'd been feeling for months had reached its breaking point and I felt ready to retch all over the ground.

"Why don't we just go home?"

She nodded. I walked to the subway, arms crossed. When the train came, I stared out the window, ignoring Heather's small talk beside me.

That night, she climbed in bed next to me and started kissing my back. I turned over and she pulled the gown over my head. She hadn't bothered to dress, and her brown nipples pointed up in the air.

We didn't need to talk. Instead, we let our mouths and hands say everything as we fed off each other. I clutched her body as I came, scared that if I let go I'd lose her forever.

The next morning, we watched TV while we waited for our parents to come.

I heard myself speak. "What's it gonna be?" Then I wished I could erase the words, because as much as I needed to know, I didn't want to hear her answer.

She pounded her leg, another nervous habit of hers. "I'll see you at school."

"As what?"

"I don't know."

I got off the couch. "Got it. Enough said."

. . . . .

I FLUSH THE toilet and leave the stall. She's waiting for me.

"Hi." Her voice is hesitant.

I wash my hands. "Hi."

"You look nice."

"Thanks." I don't intend to make this easy for her.

She starts fidgeting. "Your mom told us about the job offer. Congrats. You'll love Houston." When I don't say anything, she continues. "I'll be in Brooklyn for a while. But I've got a place of my own now."

I really wish I could make small talk like she's trying to, but there's too much past between us for that. None of it easy or perfect, but too deep to reduce to a conversation on job offers and outfits.

I catch her eye through the mirror and watch as she hesitantly steps closer to me. "Maybe I could visit sometime."

My body still yearns for her, but I'm trying to remain as impassive as possible. To distract myself, I pull out my lip pencil and fix my mouth, even though it doesn't really need it. "Oh, I don't know. What would your parents think?"

"It's not their choice." She stares at me now, more confident. "I told them that."

I whirl around, my promise to remain composed forgotten. "Really?"

"Yeah, well, not everything. But enough."

"How'd they take it?"

She shrugs. "They didn't disown me. That's a start, I guess. But she still expects grandchildren."

She giggles and I realize just how much I've missed her. Not just the sex, but her laughter and corny jokes and every other quirky thing about her.

Her gaze is serious now. "I miss you. I've been such an ass, but I want my best friend back. I want my girlfriend back. I couldn't let you leave without knowing that."

It's the first time she's ever called me that—her girlfriend. Our past wasn't perfect, but her words right now are. But still I stay silent, staring into her green eyes, drinking in the uncertainty lurking within them.

We hear a bell. It's time to line up. I pull open the door. "After you." As she walks through, I grab her arm. "I want a blue plate set. A good one."

I can't tell whether she wants to slap me or cry. "What?"

"My housewarming gift. Bring it when you visit."

She squeals and throws her arms around me, until I'm gasping for breath. "I thought you were gonna say no." She kisses me, hard. "I love you."

"I love you too." I untangle myself and push her through the door. "But don't forget my plates."

RETURNING TO MY SENSES: 2001-2002

KAREN TAYLOR

WHEN YOU LIVE in a place that everyone else in the world wants to visit, you get lazy. You can always visit this landmark or that romantic venue tomorrow. Or next week. That's how, after living in the Big Apple all my life, I'd never managed to make it to Windows on the World. We had even made reservations for New Year's Eve on the millennium, but Lorraine came down with a horrible case of the flu, and we had canceled the reservation, and then somehow never got around to making a new one.

Now, we never would.

After that terrible day in September, Lorraine and I stayed closer to home. We loved traveling, and over the years we visited the great cities of Europe, cruised the Mediterranean, traveled through Central America, and even took one foray to the Far East. True xeno-philes, we loved touring, sampling exotic flavors, and meeting amazing people. But to leave our beloved city now seemed incomprehensible. We needed to be home; needed to be among the millions of strangers who were now our comrades, all of us learning to live in this new world together.

In unspoken agreement, we chose the first weekend we could pull ourselves away from the safety of our Queens apartment to visit a place that seemed the least damaged by the terror: the Bronx Zoo. We walked down the paths, listening to the sounds of the birds and beasts, their ordinary noises helping us forget the utter silence above us, in a clear blue September sky usually full of jets taking off and landing at the nearby airports. We passed families, the children chattering, parents as quiet as we were, some anxiously looking skyward at the unmistakable roar/whoosh of F-16s, others exchanging glances of camaraderie and shared pain as we all strolled aimlessly. Lorraine and I held hands, tentatively at first, watching the fish swim plac-idly beneath us, walking back through the tree-lined pathways filled with songbirds and sparrows. Walking through the Botanical Garden back toward the subway, the sounds shifted back, slowly but surely, to the noise of street traffic and children playing. I was crying by the time we got on the subway, leaning against Lorraine's shoulder as she quietly comforted me.

It was after that trip to the Bronx that Lorraine and I

decided not to stop being tourists. We would just do it differently. New York City was now even more precious a place, and a jewel whose many facets we had not thoroughly explored. We would tour, eat new foods, indulge in our delight of different cultures, without ever getting too far away from a ride home on the subway or bus. Bringing back a sense of our normal routine allowed me to sleep through the night for the first time in weeks. I woke with Lorraine's arm across me, realizing it had also been that long since we had stopped touching.

There is only one subway that doesn't travel through Manhattan, so we chose to use it for our next excursion. Eventually, we ended up in Brighton Beach, known also these days as Little Odessa. In the still warm days of autumn 2001, we walked the world famous Boardwalk, facing out into the dark gray waters of the Altantic, away from the city's skyline. We strolled slowly down the Boardwalk, navigating around moon-faced grandmothers in kerchiefs, lanky young men lounging against pay phones, past a playground filled with shouting children and young mothers, as well as a crowd of old men crouched over a chessboard. Finally, with the beach and ocean before us, we stopped in at Tatiana's, one of the dozens of Russian restaurants with open seating facing the water. Food for me had been merely nourishment for weeks, and I was hoping that blinis and vodka would remind me of some of the other pleasures that seemed so far away lately. I ordered a variety of dishes for the table, and sat back, admiring the view, and my lover.

Lorraine was the quintessential New Yorker: part Puerto Rican, part Italian, with a Queens accent. Her dark eyes were fringed with thick lashes, her lips full and so kissable. Her skin was a light honey color that darkened to show its Mediterranean heritage in the summer. And me, with a Greek name but genes mostly hailing from Western Europe, I stayed a bland pale color all year around, without any of the haughty beauty of the Russian and Ukrainian blondes around us. But I didn't care. With Lorraine by my side, I was queen of the world. And here we were, living in a city that brought the world to us. We toasted each other with shots of vodka, nibbling at caviar and biting the heads off of shrimp served in a tart sauce. My taste buds reawakened with the mesh of flavors . . . Had I even known that my sense of taste had gone dormant? Did I remember what Lorraine tasted like? We strolled down to the beach, our fingers tangling themselves together as the water threw itself against the sand. Lorraine told me stories of earlier summers on the beach, when her teenage cousins would meet questionable dates in the shadows under the Boardwalk. She smiled when I dared to ask if she ever met anyone there, to grope through adolescence in cool shadows on the beach. She didn't answer, but the smile was enough. I kissed her smile as the sun set, casting long shadows of our bodies across the sands. The taste of her, infused with shrimp and vodka, relaxed me—we could talk, even smile about sex again.

As our city began to reexamine itself, Lorraine and I did the same. One gray Sunday in October, we traveled into Astoria, where I grew up, and I took her into St. Irene's, which was filled with bearded, virile priests chanting in Greek and comforting the sobbing grandmothers who had not yet succumbed to America's Protestant hesitation in the face of demonstrative Orthodox immigrant emotions. After the service, we waded through the musk of frankincense and sandalwood and I showed Lorraine the weeping icon, a glittering relic worshipped in the dusky Byzantine church, here in the land of fast cars and dot-coms. Her fingers brushed lightly against the ropes of pearls fastened around the icon, my eyes following their path until they seemed to disappear again into the murky haze—lacing her fingers through mine as the silence seemed to envelop us. A silence broken, by my beloved, with a loud, very undignified sneeze! I blinked, then laughed, meeting her dancing eyes with a grin as people around us blessed Lorraine over and over again, then wrapped my arm around her shoulders to lead her outside. We both sucked in a breath, then Lorraine sneezed again, laughing at the more familiar scent of exhaust fumes and streetside gyro stands.

We headed over the Grand Central Parkway to the newer immigrant community in the neighborhood—the Egyptians. Many of the coffee shops and bakeries were nearly empty, a sign of the enormous fear and mistrust resting heavily over the city. We passed a richly decorated door with an Eye of Horus painted over it, and the smell of Egyptian coffee wafted to the street. A comforting scent for anyone raised in a Mediterranean home, I actually paused for a moment. It was Lorraine who spotted the smiling, round man with an apron wrapped around his body in the doorway beneath the Eye. He nodded warmly to us, opening his hands in a welcoming gesture. Enchanted by his delight in seeing us, we let him lead us to a table, where we dipped filo into sesame-infused sauces, eagerly ate the lamb sausage known as mombar, and enjoyed the lightly seasoned vegetables and rice. Resting against elaborately decorated cushions, we stole a kiss as the owner of the restaurant presented a special dessert of pears wrapped in filo dough atop a fruit compote. That night, back at home, I licked the remnant of pomegranate syrup from Lorraine's lips, and we made love for the first time since early September.

In the warm fall days of late October, the bridges and tunnels connecting the many parts of New York City slowly reopened. Lorraine chose to surprise me with a drive over the Verrazano Bridge to the least-noticed borough of the city, once the butt of jokes and now infamous for housing the remains of the Twin Towers at one of its giant landfills. Staten Island also houses a Confucian garden, one of only a handful in the entire country. Her hips swaying provocatively in a saffron-colored skirt, Lorraine led me through carefully crafted grottos, past the peaceful, chrysanthemum-laden flower beds, into a shelter surrounded by trees that I was sure would be filled with blossoms in the spring. This time Lorraine took the lead, wrapping herself around me, her hands clasping my buttocks to pull me closer to her, into her, surrounding me with comfort and passion and color.

When winter finally came to the Big Apple, I took Lorraine to Jackson Heights for that year's subdued Diwali, the Hindu Festival of Lights. We visited the Indian sweet shops and then I bought Lorraine gold bangles from a sari-draped woman just a little darker than my lover; her sweet smile warmed us more than the masala we had had for dinner. Taking advantage of the odd geography New York makes of the world, I took Lorraine around the corner from Little India and crossed Roosevelt Avenue heading a few blocks into Woodside, where my favorite lesbian bar was pounding out salsa and meringue. We slid around each other, Lorraine sometimes spinning away from me, her hips swaying to the music of her childhood and adolescence. Dancing, we lost ourselves there for a few hours, grinding against each other in rhythm, continuing even when the music ended. It took us only a few beats to get home and continue our grinding in earnest. We were demanding now, in our desire for each other, clawing to get closer, urgently pulling our tongues and fingers in deeper, trying to find that place that seemed so easy to access just a few months ago. We fell asleep exhausted, wrapped tightly still.

February for us usually meant an annual trip to Chinatown for dim sum and illegal fireworks bursting in the shadow of the Towers. But I still didn't think I could bear it, so Lorraine took me past Shea Stadium and into Flushing, where the Taiwanese, Korean, Vietnamese, Chinese, and Japanese communities celebrated the Year of the Horse together, here in a land that lumped them all into one "Asian" community. We let ourselves be assimilated, too, waving red and gold flags as veterans, children, politicians, and civic groups followed the enormous dragon down Main Street. I sampled a fruit shake with tapioca pearls which popped in my mouth as I sucked them through the straw, making me laugh with simple joy and pleasure. We strolled through Flushing Meadows Park, passing families from around the world gathered to watch the pick-up soccer games and the multicolored teenagers flirting in the gardens near the museum, and let the sun lead us home, watching it set over the fragile skyscrapers of Manhattan. Lorraine undressed me, kissing my mouth, my neck, my breasts, my belly, my cunt, taking her time. I felt the orgasm build through my muscles, bursting out of me, washing over Lorraine as well, releasing me in ways I hadn't realized had been bound for so long.

One Sunday around Easter I took Lorraine into Manhattan for the first time in months. As far away as we could be from what was known to the world as Ground Zero, we walked the streets of Harlem, heading to Sylvia's for soul food before the churches let out. We lingered over fried catfish and collard greens, watching the parade of hats on beautiful women of all sizes and ages as they came through the doors, greeting friends and family. I don't remember when or how the music started, but a small band was playing in a hidden corner. Voices rich in joy and sorrow filled the room as we all sang hallelujahs, clapping our hands and rocking from side to side. When we reluctantly gave up our table and waded back through the crowd and out to the sidewalk, Lorraine continued to sing. Old men smiled and young children joined in, following us happily to the end of the block as we half-strolled, half-danced our way down the boulevard.

In March, we returned to the ocean, this time to Coney Island. It was not yet warm enough for the beach, and the sun was already casting slanted shadows by the time the old subway rattled into the station, but we joined a lusty crowd of locals heading into Luna Park, eating cotton candy and Nathan's hot dogs. Steering past the old wooden rollercoaster and the skee ball palaces, I pulled Lorraine toward the Wonder Wheel. Once the tallest structure in New York City, half of the Wonder Wheel's cars are fixed, but half are hooked on rails that allow the chairs to suddenly slide forward and back, as the giant wheel ascends and descends. Lorraine and I slid into one of the movable cars, as giddy as teenagers. As the stately wheel began its rise, I kissed Lorraine passionately, and slid my hand under her skirt. She giggled, and just as my fingers touched her lacey underwear, the car slid suddenly forward, throwing me off balance, and making Lorraine shriek and throw her arms around me. We laughed for joy, as the garish lights of the park below us flicked on and the sounds of the carnival grew dimmer, and she tickled me as the car swung again. Giggling wildly, I held her closer and slid her panties off, and she wiggled closer to me, spreading her thighs and pulling my head down to her breasts. I slid fingers into her wetness as Lorraine pulled aside her sweater to give me better access to her nipples. I hungrily tugged at them with my lips and my free hand as Lorraine pushed herself against my knuckles, rubbing her clit across my fingers. I pushed a third finger into her slick cunt and Lorraine moaned, holding her breasts forward so I could more quickly suck and nibble at her nipples in the rapid pattern she enjoyed. Then unexpectedly, the car moved again, slamming backward on its rail, dislodging my mouth and fingers. I tumbled to the floor of the car giggling, as Lorraine gasped in frustration. I remained where I was, pushing her skirt away, and burying my laughter in her warm cunt, licking and sucking at her clit. I knew from the strangled, hungry noises she was making that Lorraine was playing with her nipples, twisting them as I brought her closer to the edge. I could hear her whimpering and grunting as she pushed herself on me, smothering me in her slick scent.

In the split second before she exploded into orgasm,

the car shifted again. This time I had braced myself so Lorraine would be pushed forward onto my fingers and mouth as she came. She writhed against me, her fingers digging into my hair to keep herself from tumbling on top of me. I gasped for breath as she finally relaxed, and pulled myself back onto the seat next to her. We were both still breathing heavily as the century-old wheel continued its stately rotation. We were still high enough to see the skyline of Manhattan, changed irrevocably. But now, two shafts of light were beaming upward, visible even here, nearly ten miles away. I gazed at them as we resettled ourselves on the seat, then turned my eyes to Lorraine, still flushed from her orgasm. And I fell in passionate love all over again, with my lover, and my city.

THERE'S NO PLACE LIKE HOME

W. S. CROSS

WHEN I WAS growing up in Philadelphia, there was an ordinance that said you couldn't erect a building taller than Billy Penn's hat. There's a statue of William Penn, the founder on the top of City Hall. *American Bandstand* was better when it was in Philadelphia, because the kids on the show could really dance. Once it moved to California, the dancing sucked because California kids have no rhythm. Philly is also the home of the cheese steak, which tastes great, but there are all kinds of rumors about which race track the meat comes from. Nobody cares, it's served on the most scrumptious soft hoagie roll you've ever tasted. Funny how I miss it. Like the soft pretzel and water ices, the cheese steak was created in South Philly, a small town in the midst of the big city, where if you walked down Passyunk Avenue, its main drag, all the stores used to have pictures of the pope, JFK and Frank Sinatra. It's where I was born and lived until I got married.

God, do I miss it some days.

My ancestors who settled in Philadelphia never left. None of them—I'm the first. And even if I'm only, comparatively speaking, "just up the road" in New York, it's still like I'm living in another world. My husband hates Philly, so we don't visit all that often. And my relatives seem to be worried that the bridges over the Delaware River will fall down while they're visiting, so they never come up to see me, except maybe on Christmas or Thanksgiving. So you can understand why it meant so much to me when Cookie came to visit.

Cookie and I had been friends in high school, even though we didn't go to the same school. I attended South Philadelphia High, which is still public, while Cookie was a "Goretti Gorilla." That's what we called the students from all-girls St. Maria Goretti High. Run by nuns, it had a dress code, religion, and everything. The good-looking girls would hike up their uniform skirts under their belts when class was over, and the ugly ones were why we called them "Goretti Gorillas."

Cookie and I knew each other through mutual friends. The most pivotal in the group was Ellen, who went to South Philly High, but was close to Cookie. I never knew how close until we got to Temple freshman year. The campus is up in North Philly, and most of us South Philly kids hung out together, playing pinochle in the student union, snacking on all the things we weren't allowed to eat in high school, figuring out who we were. College was the first time I ever found out about gay people. Oh, I'd read about "homosexuals" in health class, and my dad made cracks about Liberace. There were also plenty of rumors about Miss Bevilaqua, the gym teacher. OK, I know that's such a cliché about dykey women gym teachers, but she was the only obviously gay person I knew; nobody else in South Philly was "gay." If they were, they didn't have the guts to let it out. South Philly was mostly Italian-American back then, and the greaser boys would have kicked the shit out of anyone, male or female, if they thought they were queer.

It was at Temple, though, that some of the kids I knew started "coming out," though sometimes the process was pretty strange. Tommy Kaufman asked me out that semester, and even tried to get me into bed. We made out on the couch a little bit, and I could feel his dick getting hard. But it was more fumble than fun for me, so we broke things off after a few dates. He never got past about second base. I didn't see Tommy after that (he was at University of Pennsylvania, so we didn't exactly share many common activities). A year or so later, I got a letter from a girlfriend who told me in passing that "Tommy's parents have come to terms with him being gay." Wow, who'd a thunk it?

Anyway, college was when I found out about Ellen and Cookie. Seems all through high school, they were a lot closer than any of us figured. As in: they were lovers. Hello! How did we miss that? Freshman year at Temple, Ellen broke things off with Cookie and immediately got engaged to Frank Evanston. I'm not sure what shocked me more: finding out Cookie and Ellen were lovers, or Ellen dropping her for an average, "safe" guy like Frank. They married the following May, and moved away to some hick town where Frank teaches in the junior high. Ellen refused even to take Cookie's phone calls; Cookie had a nervous breakdown and dropped out of Temple for a semester.

I was already gone by then: seems you are likely to flunk out of college if you cut all your classes to play pinochle in the student union. I wasn't ready for college—wasn't ready for much of anything. I got married, followed my husband to New York where he worked on Wall Street, and found a pretty good job in Manhattan. Then one day Cookie writes me and asks how I'm doing. I call her up, and it's just like no time had passed at all. We chatted about old friends, new friends, South Philly, and pretty soon, she was hinting about coming to New York for a visit.

After I got off the phone, my husband told me my South Philly accent had come back. I had worked really hard to lose it when I moved away. New Yorkers look down on Philadelphians. Instead of getting defensive, I grinned and asked him, "Yo, who ya tawkin' about?"

The day of Cookie's arrival, I was as nervous as a bride-to-be, bustling all over the apartment straightening things up two or three times. Finally the intercom rang and I buzzed her into the building. I didn't wait for her to knock at my door, instead meeting her at the top of the stairs.

"Fran, how ya been?"

My name's Francesca, but nobody in South Philly goes by their given name. Everything gets shortened: Anthony becomes Ant-nee, Tony becomes Tone, Katherine is either Cassie or Kate, and Francesca became "Fran." Nobody in New York calls me Fran, not even my husband, only people from South Philly. My voice was cramped and I had trouble getting my words out. So I just yelled her name.

"Cookie!"

Cookie looked different than I remembered her. She was never the most feminine girl in the group, but wasn't mannish. Not what I expected from a lesbian. If anything, she had the body and face of a little boy, with dark skin and shiny black curly hair. She was dressed in slacks and a silk shirt, and I could tell even before I hugged her that she wasn't wearing a bra. Didn't need one, her smallish breasts were firm and didn't jiggle all that much when she walked.

After I'd closed the door and put her things in the bedroom, we sat down on the couch and just talked. It was so good to feel relaxed and not have to pretend I was a sophisticated New Yorker. We talked about "back home," like how her mother had sold the house on Sartain Street and moved to Cherry Hill to live with Cookie's sister and brother-in-law, or how she had a studio in Center City and was living alone. After I filled her in on my family in Philly, she grabbed my arm and asked, "Whadya say we go out tonight, just the two of us?"

Seems Cookie had a couple of lesbian bars she wanted to scope out, and so we decided we'd have a late dinner and then go barhopping. My husband, Bruce, usually works late, even on Fridays. What the hell, she was the first person from Philly not related to me to come to New York. It sounded like fun.

"Sure." I grinned so hard I felt tears in the corners of my eyes. "I know a cool Thai restaurant a few blocks from here."

"We don't want to arrive too early. The crowds don't get good at most women's bars until around midnight."

The first place we went was smoky and crowded with masculine-looking women in leather; the second one reminded me of a poor attempt at dinner theater in the round, with too many gay males preening and showing off. Cookie seemed to know what she wanted, and it was all like touring a foreign country to me. The third place was at the bottom of a long staircase, and was called Jody's. It seemed like any other trendy New York watering hole I'd been to—minus any men. As in not one. All the women were dressed in smart casual clothes.

"Wow," Cookie crowed, "this looks like we hit the jackpot."

I admit I was a bit nervous now that we'd settled in. What if someone tried to pick me up—or worse, pick up Cookie and leave me all alone? But evidently they assumed we were together, and so that's how it ended up: we danced, drank, and talked for what seemed like hours without anyone disturbing us. She brought me up-to-date on all the goings-on with the old crew, including a few who'd come out of the closet, and even spoke about Ellen.

"It's been hard at times." She lowered her eyes and wasn't smiling for almost the first time all night. "But I'm better off without her. She never would go anywhere someone might see us. And honestly, she was far from the greatest lover I've ever had. I like someone who takes the initiative and doesn't just lie there like a limp dish rag."

In spite of our being in a lesbian bar, that was the one and only mention of sex the whole night. The rest of the time we just talked about Philly, how much I missed it, how small and smothering it was for her. I wondered if maybe we should switch places, but Cookie looked right through me.

"You're really lucky being here, Fran. You might not realize it, but you are. What with Bruce and the whole world at your feet. You just wouldn't be happy back home."

Home. I wondered about what she said, but then another great oldie started up and we got to dancing. We'd been dancing most of the night, and I felt that warm flush of energy that you get when you're having fun and feeling the electricity of a new place. I could have kept going, but after a few hundred more turns around the floor, I saw her yawn. It was getting late, and we decided to head back to my apartment.

At the top of the club's steep staircase, Cookie turned around, and caught me as I came up behind her, putting a hand on my shoulder. Before I could say anything, she put her arm around my neck, drew me to her, and kissed me hard on the lips. At first I started to push her away, surprised—afraid, too, that I would fall backward down the steps and into the depths of the lesbian world. But her lips were soft and tender, and I felt myself melting with each second we continued in that clench. My labia began to moisten perceptibly, and I could feel a huge flush come over me as I realized how much I liked it, liked that it was Cookie.

We didn't linger, instead she grabbed my hand and skipped outside where we hailed a cab back to my neighborhood. We found a small café still open, and had coffee while we talked some more. Gingerly reaching for my hand, she gently rubbed the back of it, and I didn't resist. Now with enough stimulation from the kiss and the caffeine to jump-start a power plant, we headed home to my apartment. Maybe a nightcap would settle down all my excess energy?

It was after two and Bruce was asleep. I forgot to leave him a note to inflate the air bed for him and me out here in the living room. We only have a one-bedroom apartment, so I wondered what to do about sleeping arrangements as I closed the bedroom door. No point waking him now. I poured us cognacs. Cookie didn't touch hers; I downed mine in one gulp.

"I was planning on giving you our bed tonight."

"It's OK," Cookie whispered, "I'm fine here on the couch."

"Are you sure?"

"Yeah, been sleeping on other people's couches for years." She smiled. There was something so guileless and genuine about that smile, so not-New York. I kept moving toward the bedroom, then moving back, sitting first on the arm of the couch, then next to Cookie as we talked and giggled.

I was fidgeting when she asked, "Can't settle down?"

"I guess I don't want the evening to end," I finally admitted.

As soon as I said it, Cookie kissed me again. This time I didn't push back and wasn't surprised. I kissed her as hard as I could, and our tongues were quickly doing all our talking in a non-verbal language. I don't know why, but it just felt "right." At first it was just kissing, but we quickly moved from making out to exploring each other's bodies through our clothes. Touching another woman like this felt naughty, and for a moment I thought of Bruce sleeping in the other room. What would he say? I'd never been untrue to him, though I'd thought about it. Just thoughts. Everyone has them, right? Only never with a woman. That it was bad made it feel all that much better.

"Hey, what's this? No bra?"

Cookie's question brought me back from my alcohol-enhanced thoughts. She was right: no bra. I'm really too big to go without one and not be obvious, so I'd worn a tight-fitting camisole under my blouse. Once she touched my breasts, though, it was obvious there was nothing underneath to prevent her from feeling their swelling mass and hardening nipples. Her touch felt so good, I didn't want her to stop.

"Who'd you wear this for?" she asked with a sly wink.

"Who do you think, silly," and I stuck my tongue into her mouth as I kissed her to shut her up. I hadn't deliberately planned things to work out this way. Really, I swear.

Pretty soon we were getting the buttons undone and the zippers unzipped, with clothes flying onto the floor. I found her smallish, firm breasts a turn-on in comparison to mine, but she didn't seem to mind their size and was soon biting my nipples. I once felt another girl's breasts in high school when she went around the gym daring us to touch them. I never could refuse a dare.

"Ouch! Be careful, I don't want to wake up Bruce."

She froze at the mention of his name, and I could see her flames dampen.

"What's the matter?"

"I feel a little funny doing this with your husband in the next room sleeping."

I thought about that, thought about whether it was wrong to do this, but I didn't think about it very long. My cunt was throbbing from all the flirting, talk, coffee, and kissing, and I could feel it wetting the fabric of the couch now that we were sitting there naked. I wrapped both arms around her neck and pulled her down to my pussy.

"I'll take that chance." She didn't resist.

Her tongue felt like a small snake striking my clit, sending shockwaves of pleasure up through my stomach and making my shoulders tremble like palsy. Her skilled fingers complemented inside my cunt the flicking motion of that tongue on my clit, until orgasm after orgasm flooded over me. At one point, I couldn't stand it any longer.

"Wait, I'm going to pass out."

Hearing this, Cookie rose up from between my legs and kissed me hard, her mouth tasting of salt and sex. It was my turn. I remembered how she disliked passive lovers. Although I'd never had sex with a woman before, I figured I would just try and imitate what she'd done to me. I lay down on the floor and pulled her on top of me, her hips over my mouth, her cunt within easy reach. She continued to lick my pussy as I worked on her lips in a perfect symmetry; if only there was someone to watch.

At first I just ran my tongue along her labia. The taste was strange, a little off-putting at first, then gradually more inviting as I got used to its muskiness. Oral sex with a man was usually stronger smelling, but like many women, I'd been raised with a hatred of "down there." My sister still douches, and my mother always warned us about "pad odor" and other terrible secretions. Why hadn't it bothered me when Cookie was eating me out? Ask my cunt that question.

"Fuck it!" I thought, and I did.

Moving past her outer lips, my tongue was soon inside the sweetness of her pussy, its moisture spreading over my mouth like a kinky milk moustache. At first I could tell I wasn't getting the hang of it, because Cookie continued to work me over in our magical 69 position. OK, what now? I thought to myself. I inserted first one and then two fingers into her pussy while moving my circling tongue up to her clit. Within seconds of this, Cookie was panting and no longer tonguing me at all.

I could feel her orgasms as they came in bunches, her pussy wetting my face, her thighs clenching, her breathing quickening into gasps. When we reached a stopping point, she rolled over and began to kiss me again. I wanted to wipe my mouth first, but she held my face and licked the moisture from our lovemaking off my lips before plunging her tongue inside.

"Let me really girl-fuck you now," she whispered in

my ear, and began pumping me with first one finger, then two, then it seemed like her whole hand. I felt myself slipping into that twilight between consciousness and reverie. Whether it was the late hour, the wine spritzers we'd had hours before, or the sex, I no longer knew quite where I was.

How many orgasms had I had tonight? I'd lost count. When I couldn't take any more, I rolled Cookie over and did my best to imitate what she'd done to me. She came in my arms violently, then peacefully, until finally we both collapsed and just lay there in our naked softness. Part of me wished someone had a camera to capture this moment of deep bliss. Not the sex, the connection: it hadn't been with just any woman, it was with Cookie.

By the time she fell asleep in my arms, it was nearly five. I gently disengaged myself, covered her with a blanket I took from the hall closet, then picked up my clothes, and tiptoed into the bedroom. After brushing my teeth and carefully making sure to wash off her scent, I slipped into bed beside Bruce, who was snoring slightly. I was surprised how I didn't feel guilty, and simply snuggled up to him in a sort of fetal position. That's when I felt his enormous hard-on pressing into my back. Before I could think about it, he was inside me, moaning.

"Ssshh!" I hissed. "You'll wake up Cookie!"

HEAT

ILSA JULE

*"Fruit cannot drop through this thick air—fruit
cannot fall into heat that presses up and blunts
the points of pears and rounds the grapes."*

MORNING, NOON, AND night, *heat*. It was
the first thing on our minds as we awakened in the
morning from troubled sleep and the last thought at
night as we descended into fitful sleep. The lines from
H.D.'s poem ran through my mind, on an endless loop.
Had she been in New York City in August when she
penned them? All those who could afford to leave
town, had. Those who remained hurried from one air-
conditioned environment to the next: home, office,
movie theater, restaurant.

My mind was cloudy, which made focusing on an

article impossible. Like a four-year-old, I pretended to read. In my damp grip was the *New York Times Magazine*. Only a few days old, it continued to wilt as I looked at it. The heat was even too much for inanimate objects. The ink moved from paper to palm and fingertips. It looked as if I had been using finger paints earlier in the day and forgot to wash up afterward. The magazine, deteriorating in my hand, was soon converted into a useful object, a fan. I waved it inches from my face. This brought no relief.

The number 6 train was delayed. Leaning forward, over the platform edge and craning my neck, I could see that it was stopped between stations. Two headlights glared down the tunnel. I stood amidst hundreds of grumpy commuters. All impatient, all hot, all standing too close together, elbowing each other. The usual level of contempt for one another was palpable, almost becoming another body among us. *It's this fucking heat!*

My hand had stopped fanning, I stared in a stupor at the track bed. It was littered with AA batteries in various states of decay. For no good reason I turned my head to the left (when I could have just as easily turned to the right) and I saw her standing several feet away on the subway platform. *Holy crap, it's Jennifer!* I sobered up in an instant (like a drunk who encounters something frightening and real) then shoved a couple of people aside as I jumped back. "Don't you know how to say excuse me?" I hid behind a tiled pillar and hoped (really prayed) to God that she hadn't seen me. I tried to ignore the pounding of my heart and the sound of blood rushing in my ears.

I thought you moved?

Steel wheels wheezed against steel track and a slow-moving train inched its way into the station. "*Oh wind rend open the heat*," I thought. Once I entered the train and found firm footing, the lenses of my glasses fogged.

If I was lucky, Jennifer had not seen me.

I heard her voice, small, behind me as she said, "Hey."

My stomach cinched and I cursed my luck. With some effort I twisted and turned. My heart ached. My pussy yearned.

"Imagine seeing you," she said, like she was genuinely happy by this accidental encounter.

"It's not that hard to imagine, is it?" I said, sarcastically, hoping she'd pick up on my tone. I planned to send her off after a brief sentence or at least by the next station stop.

I worked to quell an eagerness to jump into bed with her. This wanting disturbed my insides considerably. I kept one hand on the overhead pole, the other held the magazine, the pages of which were stiffening in the now cooler climate of the subway car.

The train started with a lurch and she fell into me, grabbing me softly around my waist. She could have righted herself but instead chose to stay pressed against me. We remained in an awkward embrace, confined by strangers. My pussy and my hands were ready for her. Although I hated to admit it, I was always ready for her. As I pulled her hands from either side of me I tossed them back to her. I wanted to kiss her fingers. At the same time I wanted her to leave me alone.

"Going somewhere?" she asked.

I noticed that her eyes were still pretty. Clear blue. They were set against skin made all the more attractive by tiny freckles. She used to get hit on by models, female models, when she lived in the city.

"Yeah. I'm going home. Alone." I said flatly.

"I'm sure your dinner is being prepared as we speak," she said, her attempt to discern whether I was single or coupled.

"No, I don't go home to a caretaker," I said sharply.

She let the barb go and said, "You moved a while ago, right?"

"Yeah," I said and looked over her shoulder. I was feeling the urge to kiss her and start an argument at the same time. She knew that I was still stuck on her.

"Where are you headed?" I asked, hoping she was transferring to another line.

She looked at me coyly and said, "Downtown."

She placed her hand on my arm. I looked at it and then into her eyes.

"So, how is Grandma Moses?" I asked and couldn't suppress the smile from my lips. I wanted to annoy her. Doing that would bring me pleasure.

"Who?" she said, looking away, falling into me slightly as the train cornered.

"You know, Suzanne," I said, drawing out the 'Zanne. When in doubt, always bring up the girlfriend, particularly if they have been together a couple of years. All the lovey-dovey stuff is over and boredom, the rot that starts to destroy the foundation of any relationship, has set in.

"She's fine," she replied. "She's tenured at Rutgers."

I made sure to look unimpressed.

Then Jenn continued. "We just got back from vacation."

I hadn't been on a proper vacation in over five years, let alone a romantic getaway. "Where'd you go?" I asked, then mentally chimed in, "Puerto Rico," as she said the words.

"And, you had fun?" I asked.

"It was okay," she said in a way that implied it was not. Then she rubbed her knuckles against her lips and batted her long eyelashes at me. She always rubbed her knuckles against her mouth when she wanted me. Once I learned to tell, I always knew when I had a winning hand or when I should fold and go home.

My attention was drawn to my own mouth, my lips were full. I chewed on my lower lip.

My heart was sore from being dumped and I thought, incorrectly, that someday I would not want her. Instead I dreamt of her and longed for her touch and felt pathetic. This was the type of thing that happened to someone in an Edith Wharton novel. This was not supposed to be my fate. I wanted to be the one to whisk her away to a foreign land. My mind flashed to the happy-tired feeling one feels after a day spent exploring a new city. I wanted to smell her skin, warmed by my touch and the sun. I wanted to rub oil into her back and calves before bed, then find a misplaced store of energy and plunge into making love.

I wished, now, that her hands I had pulled from my waist were still resting there. I took a small step, almost imperceptible, toward her and pressed my arm against her. She didn't move away. We remained pressed together, gently. The last time we had been this close was during a crowded holiday office party after she had broken things off. After an hour of milling around and a few drinks down our gullets we stood, close, like this. Even then she'd been with 'Zanne. I had mixed feelings when she quit work to go to grad school. I wasn't entirely relieved when she had gone.

Now, weary evening commuters imposed us upon each other.

Over Jenn's shoulder I watched a mother, flanked by her two boys, seated next to where we stood. One boy about age seven read to his mother from a book, while his younger brother, who couldn't read, got attention by making faces. "Mamí, look," he said. I laughed when she exclaimed, "*Que feo*," as he scrunched his face, crossed his eyes, and stuck out his tongue between his first set of teeth.

As we detrained and waited on the platform at Union Square Jenn whispered, "I want you to fuck me."

My fingers were gleeful at the thought. My pussy was a fist ready to get into a fight.

"Don't mess with me," I said, angered, and pulled away from her. She stepped toward me and whispered, "No, baby. I need you to fuck me." She tugged at the belt loop of my pants.

I whispered into her ear, "I'm not your girlfriend." Recycling the line she had used on me during the months we spent sleeping together.

Then I knew I could look her in the eye.

Annoyed, she hissed, "You're no fun."

For a minute I wondered what grade we were in and then a smile started to pull at the corners of my mouth.

"Don't even think of saying I told you so," she said and leaned into me. I felt my legs get a little unsteady.

"All right," I whispered, as a homeless man shuffled by lugging a large clear plastic bag full of empty cans, leaving an oily trail behind him. "I'll fuck you, but I get to be in control."

She mulled this over. She hated to lose control. Her battles with anorexia attested to that.

"Fine," she said and then became quiet.

We fell into a silence then boarded the 5 train. Our bodies swayed back and forth as the train headed full speed beneath the East River into Brooklyn. I leaned over and inhaled a sense of her. The way she smelled had been the first thing I liked about her. I think she wore an expensive leave-in hair conditioner. My hair, cropped short, hadn't suffered a split end or case of the frizzies, ever. I came to know of hair care products through the women I slept with.

At Borough Hall I looked at her and she looked back.

"My mother was killed," she stated flatly.

I hid my surprise, knowing she wanted to get a reaction out of me. Jenn liked to draw you into her drama so that she wouldn't have to take responsibility for her part in it. It was the listener who was supposed to have all the feelings so she didn't have to.

I never know what you are supposed to say when someone says something like that. My first thought was to ask if the boyfriend had done it even though I had imagined her mother as the one who should have killed him. The lying, cheating creep went so far as to leave other women's panties in the coffee maker, in the kitchen!

Should I offer some words of sympathy or support? I wanted details, something to write about in my journal. I didn't want emotions connected to any of this, least of all her mother whom I had never met.

"That's awful," I said and touched her shoulder. Touching her had always been confusing. It still was.

Jenn continued. "She was killed by a drunk driver, upstate."

I knew she wished it had been the boyfriend and I

said, "It's always the good ones. Too bad—"

She cut me off. "Yeah, he's such a fucking prick," and her eyes grew dark for a moment. The same darkness that pervaded them when she was in a blackout.

I draped an arm around her shoulders and pulled her close to me. Even in boots, which she was wearing that day, she was petite. I suddenly felt very large. I pressed my lips to the top of her head and gave her a small kiss. She never wanted people to know we were lovers when we had been together and now that we weren't she seemed to want to lead them to that conclusion.

As we approached Nevins Avenue, I said, "We have to catch the local. C'mon." She rolled her eyes to indicate "Another train?" I nudged her out the door with a thrust from my hips.

The multitude of putrid smells of the station were amplified in the humidity. We walked toward the back of the platform, careful to avoid something that dripped from the ceiling. She didn't let go of my hand. All my little worries—*Why am I doing this? Who was I? Was I good enough?*—scurried about the perimeters of my esteem. Being physically close to people forced me to experience a heightened sense of self-criticism which bordered on self-loathing.

I observed the men on the platform scope her out as we walked past. I was invisible. She wore a dark skirt and dark blouse. If you didn't know any better you would never guess she was gay. They looked at her ass, her legs, and tried to make eye contact. She ignored them and pressed close to me. I telepathically gloated to all of them, *Suckers, she's going home with me.*

There on the platform, she stood on her tiptoes and gave me a small kiss on the mouth. She used to tell me she loved me each day. Yet we were failed at the outset and knew it, and in a way this drew us toward each other. Nothing could deter me from climbing into bed with her. Then or now.

As we boarded the train for our last leg, although there was plenty of room to sit, we stood together, pressed in close.

"Should we stop and get some stuff from the store?" I asked as we disembarked at my stop.

"Sure, but I'm not that hungry," she said.

"Well, you know me, if I miss a feeding I get grumpy."

She laughed, rubbed her hand against my stomach and asked, "Where does it go?"

"That is the riddle of the Sphynx," I replied.

As we stepped into the bodega at the top of the station steps I considered her anorexia. She knew how many grams of fat were in all types of food. I had studied her during meals at restaurants, of which there were few, and over time she would only meet me in bars, very late at night. I often wondered how it felt for her when she ate, but dared not ask.

I grabbed a baguette, brie, bottled water, and a few oranges.

As we stood in line behind a few other people, I unwrapped a Hershey's bar, broke off a small piece, and fed it to her. When we got to the register I received a look of contempt as I placed the open candy bar on the counter. The daughter of the owner did her math homework, seated in the storefront window next to a display of plastic fruit. As the woman rang up the order, Jenn gave me another small kiss on the mouth. I realized that I was someone who could get by on emotional crumbs.

As we entered the apartment I ushered her into the bedroom.

"You can put your clothes on that chair," I said, pointing to a wooden chair that was already covered by my clothes.

"Oh, that's romantic," she sneered. "Am I just going to take off my clothes and you'll fuck me?" Her voice was full of resentment.

"Basically," I replied. I liked to piss her off.

I headed down the long corridor to the kitchen. As I dusted off a bottle of red wine and uncorked it, I realized I couldn't remember purchasing it. I poured a glass. I only drank around her. And she should have avoided drinking all together.

I kicked off my shoes. Barefoot, I walked quietly back to the bedroom. I stood outside the door and watched her reflection in the full-length mirror. When she was under the covers I stepped into the room.

"It's fucking stifling in here. Don't you have AC?"

she asked.

"No. But they say it might snow," I said sarcastically and turned on the fan.

"Snow? In August? Hmmm, that would be nice," she said, and rubbed her hands across her body, stretching out between the sheets.

Looking at her in my bed I could have knocked myself over with a feather. There she was, like she belonged there. There she was as I had imagined her so many times. She was so fucking adorable when she was in bed.

I walked to the edge of the bed and handed her the glass of wine.

She took a sip and said, "I *love* red wine."

"I know," I said.

Once she told me that I knew nothing about her. In my own defense I thought, *I do know about you.* But the only things I could think of were the way she took her coffee and that she liked nonfat frozen yogurt, which was what she ate for lunch every day. "You refuse to let me know you," I retorted. She smiled at me and offered no hints.

Now I stood next to the head of the bed and pulled the sheet down so that her breasts were exposed. They were full C cups with brown nipples jutting skyward.

"You've got great tits," I said.

I bent down, sucked one of her nipples, watched it get hard, and asked, "Do you have to be home at any particular time?"

"Unh unh," she murmured, and put her hand on the back of my head pulling my face back to her breast.

My clit was swelling. I pulled my head back. *Had she been lying to me? Was she single or coupled?* I wanted to fuck her as 'Zanne's girlfriend. There was no remorse in my heart on that count. I wanted to hurt the one who had hurt me.

"Why not? Doesn't 'Zanne care about where you are?" I asked.

"She does, but she's not in the city today. She's at a conference in D.C."

"And she won't be hurrying back on a late train or anything like that?" I asked.

"She's not a romantic."

Lucky her, I thought.

"What are you gonna tell her?" I asked, sitting on the edge of the bed.

She took my hand and started playing with my fingers.

"Oh, I dunno. That I went out to dinner with Cal." She rubbed my fingertips against her mouth.

I winced. Names were painful reminders of the life that didn't include me. I knew Cal, she was one of those girly-girl lesbians who doesn't talk to butches. Cal was also an upper middle-class, failed actor/writer type, who waited tables and managed to live in a gorgeous one-bedroom apartment in Greenwich Village (but never admitted that Mommy and Daddy subsidized the rent).

I pressed her hand to my mouth. Then bit a knuckle.

When I kissed her hard on the mouth, which tasted of wine, she bit my lips. I knew she'd leave bruises all over my body. She wasn't gentle in bed.

"Roll over," I said and she obeyed.

I removed my work shirt and let it rest at the foot of the bed. I pulled down the sheet to reveal her broad back, covered in the same small freckles that were on her face. She thought the shape of her back was unattractive. I could have mistaken her for a high school swimmer from this angle. I pulled a bottle of massage oil from under the bed. I warmed a dab of it in my palm and then let it dribble on her back.

I rubbed it into her skin. The funny thing was, as much as I loved touching her I loved watching my hands touching her more. *You're still mine*, I thought triumphantly. I searched her pores, looking for flaws. I rubbed her back for a long time, neither of us talking. The whirring of the fan blades filled what would have been a heavy silence. Her skin was not soft; she had spent too much time in the sun and it was already getting tough. I was covered in sweat, a mixture of fear and longing.

"Is that okay?" I finally asked.

"It's perfect," she said.

I thought, *Perfect? There's really no need to embellish.*

I stood up, walked over, and turned off the light.

"It sure is dark in here," she said.

"I know, it's great for sleeping," I said.

I walked to the window and let the shade up. Some light from the street transformed things into silhouettes.

Then I worried if she would want to spend the night afterward. One thing more difficult than sleeping, was sleeping with someone else in the bed.

I slipped out of my pants and crawled over her. I left my briefs on. I felt her hands touching my legs.

"Aren't you going to take these off?" she asked, pulling at my underwear.

"Later," I said, and my T-shirt made a small, soft noise as it landed on the floor.

I pressed into her back and felt her smooth warmth. I wrapped my arms around her shoulders and rested my head between her shoulder blades. She felt just like she had before. I was surprised that a certain tenderness could still be felt between us. I thought perhaps time or her girlfriend would have erased it.

"Fuck, you feel great," I said.

I reached up, grabbed a handful of her hair, and bit the back of her neck.

She groaned and ran her fingers against the buzz cut at the base of my skull. She tried to get a hold of some of it.

"There's nothing to grab hold of," she said.

She pulled my face to hers and started kissing me. She sucked on my lips, hard. Once she gave me a hickey on my lower lip, which had been nearly impossible to explain away. Questions about the origin of the bruise went unanswered.

She said, "I've missed having your fingers inside me."

"Hmmm," was all I said.

I sat up, my eyes now adjusted to the dark, and surveyed her back and ass. I felt my clit getting hard and I reached between the wall and the bed.

"What are you doing?" she asked.

"Nothing, yet," I said and fumbled around until my fingers found the bag.

I pulled up the package. Inside the clear plastic wrapper was a cock that had never been used. I hate using the same dildo on different women. I suppose a real penis must lack all shame. Or at least be able to admit that it lacks originality.

Perhaps I was fooling myself into thinking that using a new dildo differentiated experiences with partners. Clearly I have a warped sense of conscience. The wrapper rustled between my fingers, buttery from the massage oil, and I struggled to open the package.

"What are you doing, opening a bag of chips?" she asked in response to all the rustling.

"No, a bag of dick," I said, my tone matter-of-fact.

She turned her head to look and see if I was telling the truth.

"Is blue your color?" I asked and the bag tore open.

There's new car smell, new sneaker smell, and new dildo smell. It had been meant for her but her abrupt departure had precluded its use. I was too particular when it came to money and toys and people and fucking. I had not been able to throw it away.

As I slipped the dildo into my briefs, pushing the head out of the Y front, the base caught on my pubic hair. I thought to myself, *Nothing up my sleeve. Presto!* and laughed.

"What's so funny?" she asked.

I replied, "Nothing's funny. You have a great ass."

I distracted her by pressing my nose against her coccyx and then delicately licked her anus. I heard her breathing change. I slid my legs on either side of her thighs.

She put her hands in front of her and wrapped her fingers around the iron bed frame. The bed had been left by the former tenant and though it had a sinister aesthetic, once the box spring and mattress had been replaced, it was comfortable. The iron posts and cross supports were perfectly suited to fasten wrists and ankles.

"I wish you hadn't run off like that," I said, no longer feeling like I had to be kind.

"Shut up and just fuck me," she said.

She raised her hips, elevating and angling them. I slid a pillow underneath her.

I slid my hand between the mattress and box spring and pulled out a packet of lube. I had many of them placed about so that one was always within reach. I twisted the tab in my teeth. This particular lube is my favorite. It feels just like pussy juice.

I squeezed the contents of the packet into my hand and ran my palm along the shaft of the dick. It felt hard and slick, more alien than human.

I kept my hand wrapped around it, my thumb on top, my fingers cupped underneath. My eyes started to roll back. I pressed my thumb into her cunt, which needed no lubricant, and then guided my prick inside. She let out a groan. I felt the walls of her pussy exert resistance, a force that held and expelled.

I moved carefully back and forth inside her. As I listened to my stomach slapping against her ass cheeks I knew I would come a lot sooner than I wanted to. I placed a hand on her shoulder and pressed into her. I rubbed my chest against her, the skin slick with oil and sweat. I insinuated that alien prick of mine as far as I could inside her. The base of it pressed into my clit.

Soon my pelvis moved of its own accord. I put my hands over her hands and squeezed my fingers around hers. I was going to come quickly, like a teenage boy. And I did.

I fell upon her, my heart pounding in my chest, sweat running in rivulets between my breasts and shoulder blades.

"I can feel your heart beating," she said.

"Unh huh," I replied and enjoyed being dead weight upon her.

After a few minutes, I said through labored breathing,

"It sure is warm in here."

"That snow would be nice right about now," she said and laughed.

I rolled off her and wiped the sweat off both of us with the sheet. I lay on my back and slid my hands down between her legs. I knew she hadn't come. I pressed my fingers inside her.

She sat up and looked at me in the half-light, then pulled my hand from her and straddled me. She rubbed her clit up and down, in her rhythm, against my stomach. She was wet and the more she rubbed against me the wetter she got. She reached back and pressed her fingers inside me, then sucked them and inserted them back into me. She did this a few times.

She continued to rub her clit against my stomach from my navel to the base of my rib cage. I watched her sucking on her fingers. I reached up and cupped her breasts in my hands.

She was one of the only women I'd ever slept with who got off on genital-to-genital contact. She parted my legs and pressed her clit into mine. With my hands on her hips I pulled her into me harder. I felt hot skin and the pain of her bones pressing into my bones. She rubbed herself against me in small movements until she started to shiver, which was the most amount of emotion she showed during orgasm. Then she pulled away abruptly.

She rolled over and started kissing me. The smell

of my pussy was on her face. I tasted it in her kisses. It smelled sweet and flowery and for a second I wanted to fuck myself. I pulled her flat on top of me. I licked her face. Her kisses were not like those from before. Now she took her time and didn't lose her breath. Perhaps she had finally realized that I could not overtake her in a kiss. Or that I might, but I would give it all back.

"I missed you," I finally said.

"I love you," she said.

While it is true you should never bet more than you can afford to lose, I had never felt more on loan than I did with her. It was as if I knew she wouldn't take me and so it made me offer more of myself. Mentally I had pleaded for her to love me, to call me her girlfriend. She never would.

I had my hands on her ass and was pulling her into me. I pressed our pubic bones together. I felt her in the pit of my stomach. I hated that she made me feel so corny. Corny and horny. That sums up the effect she had on me. It was pure schmaltz. Damn, I hated that she did this to me.

She said, "I'm so wet, it's embarrassing."

I almost didn't care about the sex. I wanted to keep her with me, I didn't want to just fuck her. I hated that she made me trade my love in for fucking.

She wanted me to feel how wet she was and guided my hands between her legs. I plunged my index finger inside and changed my mind. I pulled my finger out and she begged, "Please—"

I put my index finger and middle finger inside her and knew that something had fallen into place; we were both finally home.

"How could you leave me, you idiot?" I asked. My aggression turned me on. I pulled my fingers out and rolled away.

"Tsk," she said, aggravated, and then, "I have to pee," as she got out of bed.

"It's down the hall, third door on the left," I informed her.

When she came back to bed she pressed her pussy against my thigh. "This place is huge. Where's your roommate?"

"I don't have one," I said. "Isn't rent stabilization fucking beautiful?" With the last words I pressed three fingers inside her.

I pressed harder and she said, "I wish you could shove your whole arm inside me."

I knew what she meant. I rolled her onto her back and kneeled over her. In that second I knew she was making up her mind to come or quit. I felt the walls of her vagina tighten around my fingers and a much braver, quieter orgasm than the first one followed.

Then I was annoyed, and not letting her think she'd won a part of my heart, I said, while she was lying beside me still and quiet, "Do you want to take a shower?"

"Why? You want to get rid of me?" she asked.

"No, you could spend the night," I said, knowing full

well she wouldn't.

She rolled onto her side and I looked at her. I remembered watching her in her sleep and knew that missing her and wanting her would endure. I closed my eyes. I felt myself falling into a dreamy half-conscious state. I wasn't going to see her to the door. I wasn't going to kiss her good-bye.

I remembered that when we fucked at her place she always changed the sheets afterward. She'd look at the rumpled, sweat-soaked sheets with disdain and when I returned from taking a piss, she'd be making the bed almost as if she were applying fresh dressing to an old wound.

As I lay there, I noticed that my building was oddly quiet. I sometimes fantasized that all my neighbors would die on the same day and before the horrible stench set in, there would be a night of complete quiet and calm. No heavy footsteps falling on the stairs, no banging of the door to the building echoing up the stairwell, no arguments wafting up the air shaft.

"Are you asleep?" she asked.

"Nah, I was just thinking."

"Oh right, your hobby," she said and sat up.

I reached out and caressed her back.

"You know this would never work," she said in response to my touch. Then she dressed in the dark.

"Thanks for saying 'hi' tonight," I said.

"Yeah, well, nothing ventured nothing gained."

"Sorry about your mom. I know she meant a lot to you."

That didn't seem like the right way to end this night. On a selfish note I added, "I still think about that afternoon when we were lying on that futon in your living room after breakfast at the Dominican place. Sometimes it seems like yesterday."

She sat at the edge of the bed. We considered each other for a moment.

She pressed her fingers to my lips. I could smell myself. This had been her gesture in parting.

She stood up and exited the bedroom. I heard the bolts as she turned them. Light from the hallway streamed into the apartment. The door closed and I heard her footsteps as she descended the stairs.

I got up, locked the door, and headed to the kitchen. I cracked dusty ice cubes into a hand towel, rolled it, pressed it against the base of my neck, and lay on the cool linoleum floor.

A neighbor's kitchen light flicked on and my skin glowed gray. I noticed hickeys on my stomach. I rubbed my fingers across them. The neighbor's light went off.

Then I heard the downstairs neighbors begin their nightly argument. It was conducted in Spanish so I never knew what was wrong but they argued right on time. It was 12:30 a.m., perhaps the hour when one of them returned home from work?

I moved to the bedroom and wrapped myself in the sheets, enveloped by the delicious smell of fuck. I

turned off the fan so that the scent and warmth pene-
trated me.

"Good night, 'Zanne. I really enjoyed fucking your
girlfriend."

I rolled onto my stomach and fell asleep as the sound
of a garbage truck rumbled around the corner.

A LOVER IS BORN

HAZEL MILLS

I NEED TO get the fuck out of town! Work has been kicking my ass for the past few months. When I decided to become a psychiatrist, I knew that I wouldn't have a lot of free time to enjoy all the money that I would be making but I never imagined that it would be this hectic. Case after case of bipolar disorder, schizophrenia, and ADHD was making me lose my own damn mind.

Gabe has been dealing with a lot of on-the-job bullshit as well and we both could definitely use some intense rest and relaxation, so we've packed our bags and we're heading out of the city with Pascal, our Golden Retriever, in tow. We bought a small house in the Hamptons a few years ago and began renovating it immediately. We worked hard to make it a place where we could go and escape the city scene. The house was going to be our private little love nest. It took a lot of money and elbow grease but now that it's finished, it was well worth it.

Gabe and I met about ten years ago at a book club that my receptionist held once a month at her house. Even though I didn't always have the time to read the monthly selections, I still enjoyed the company and conversation. The group was a gumbo of people of all ages and backgrounds. There were housewives, a teacher, a veterinarian, and a marketing professor, just to name a few. One of the members was a sommelier for a local restaurant and he would always bring excellent wines for us to taste and, of course, we were more than happy to oblige. We would just chill and enjoy each other and catch up on the latest gossip.

Gabe was one of the few people in the group who would have actually read the selection every month and looked forward to discussing its every detail. The book discussions usually only lasted for about an hour but we would eat, drink, and be merry for far longer.

Although Gabe and I had not been formally introduced, there was something electric between us and I sensed that we both felt it. We would exchange long glances and shy smiles during the evening, flirting. I knew that I wanted and needed to know more about this intriguing character and it wasn't long before the perfect opportunity presented itself.

The club members were trying to decide on a venue for our Christmas party. We wanted to reserve the private dining room at an exclusive Japanese restaurant but we were late in planning this year's event and the place was booked solid. So I suggested that we have the party at my house. I had just finished refurbishing a brownstone uptown and wanted to show it off. At least, that was the reason I wanted them to believe.

Everyone agreed that I could host this year's party so I dusted off my hostess skills. I had not hosted a party in a very long time and had grossly underestimated the amount of work involved. I was glad that I could afford to call in reinforcement if needed and it would be worth every dime if I got what I really wanted out of the deal: Gabe. Since there was no book to discuss this month, Gabe and I would be able to talk about other things and get to know each other better. Having the party here would make my prowl more natural; I was on my own turf and Gabe was my prey.

I planned the party to be an evening of casual elegance. I hired an excellent caterer to serve a menu of culinary delights. As a favor, my designer had the house overrun with beautiful poinsettias and a tree that rivaled the one at Rockefeller Center, and the ivories in my library were being tickled by a student from the local school of the arts. Everything was perfect! Once the guests began to arrive, I realized that all of this elaborateness would be in vain if Gabe didn't show up. Thankfully, I didn't have to worry about that because just as I had started to give up hope, the doorbell rang, and it was Gabe.

"Merry Christmas and welcome to my home. I'm

Laila," I said.

"Feliz Navidad. I'm Gabriella."

I couldn't believe that she was actually in my home. My heart was racing as I considered all the possibilities that the evening held. Gabe walked graciously inside followed by an intoxicating scent of Chanel No. 22. She was truly the most beautiful woman I had ever seen. Gabe made Halle Berry look like Shaq in drag. She had her hair pulled back into a sexy ponytail that hung well past her shoulders, letting a few carefree strands dangle around her face. Her caramel skin glowed flawlessly in the candlelight.

"Let me take your coat."

"Gracias. Thank you. You have a spectacular home. How long have you lived here?" she asked as she walked slowing through the foyer, admiring the eclectic mix of art and antiques.

"Oh, about three years," I answered.

I watched her tall slender form stroll effortlessly from room to room, peaking inside and commenting on some of my Aztec pieces. Damn she was fine! She had a body that made a sister want to scream!

"Come into the parlor and say hello to everyone, get a drink, and have a look around," I encouraged. I hoped that she would especially take a liking to the master bedroom on the third floor because I was looking forward to us spending a lot of fabulous times there.

The party went off without a hitch. Everyone enjoyed sitting down at the two large round tables that were set up in the dining room and eating a traditional gourmet Christmas dinner by the fire. Gabe and I sat together and laughed and talked all evening. I was aroused just by the sound of her smoky voice. I learned that she was a divorced detective. Her chosen profession was the reason for the demise of her marriage. Her husband was content when she was just a beat cop but when she became a detective and her work grew intense, things quickly deteriorated. They didn't have any children, so once the ties were severed, they were severed for good, and she hadn't heard from him since. I also found out that her family was originally from Puerto Rico. They moved to Miami when she was five and then here when she was in high school. I sat and listened to her every word, captivated.

Gabe and a few others lingered on a while after the party for a rousing game of bid whist, but after a couple hours of being spanked by Gabe and me, the others left me and my skilled partner alone. She offered to stay and help with some of the clean up. I knew that there was no real reason for her to help with anything because Chandra, my housekeeper, was due here tomorrow morning, but I welcomed the opportunity to have her all to myself. While we filled the dishwasher, we continued to talk like two old girlfriends who'd known each other since we were in pigtails.

Then, there it was. That awful awkward silent moment that we all hate and that very few people know how to handle effectively. The knowledge that Gabe had been married made me a little concerned about whether or not she would even be down for what I had in mind. There was only one way to find out.

"Gabe, may I ask you a personal question?" I said, moving closer to where she was standing.

"Sure. Go ahead," she answered.

"Are you dating anyone right now?"

I hoped that after asking this question, I wouldn't have to listen to her go on and on about some fine-ass man on the force that she was head over heels in love with.

"No. Unfortunately not. I haven't dated a lot since the divorce. It seems that once most men find out what I do for a living, their pelotas shrink," she explained.

I laughed and decided to move on to the next question.

"How do you feel about women?"

"What do you mean?" she asked, with a suspicious tone in her voice.

"Are you into women?" I asked.

I was a bit nervous because I didn't want to offend or make her uncomfortable in any way but she seemed not at all surprised by my curiosity. I had been out since medical school so virtually everyone knew that I was a lesbian. I didn't try to hide my lifestyle at all nor did I wear it on my sleeve. I was often approached by men and would only inform them that I liked my apples stemless if they didn't easily take no for an answer. As a teenager, I never dated boys. I had guys who were friends that I hung out with but not as a couple. I just wasn't into them. It took a while for me to understand why until one of the guys was talking to me about how he and his girlfriend fucked in the backseat of his car on prom night. There was a tingle between my legs at the image of the girl lying there topless and spread eagle. I realized that I wanted to fuck a girl, too. At first, I was a bit confused at my discovery because I didn't fit the stereotypical lesbian profile that people would whisper about and point to on the street. There was nothing butch about me. I was very soft and feminine. I kept this newfound info on the DL, so to speak, until I went away to college and had my first REAL experience that confirmed what I had been feeling all along. My nana, who'd raised me since I was two, died of cancer my sophomore year. She never verbally confirmed that she knew about my homosexuality, but I think she knew. She always taught me that honesty was the highest form of self-preservation. She would say that if a person will lie to themselves about who they are and what they want, they will certainly lie to everyone else about anything. My mother decided that two years of raising a child was quite enough so she left and went only God knows where with God knows whom. I would get a birthday card from her every other year, always a day late and never with a return address. So, I was free to live my life the way I wanted. My last lover was still in the closet and wasn't interested in coming out at any time this side of the apocalypse. Her husband was a minister and she wanted to avoid the extra drama. After months of sneaking around, I realized that I deserved someone who could be open about her love for me no matter who was watching. I also wanted someone who didn't come with a ton of baggage. Life was too short to live hiding out, so we stopped seeing each other.

"No one has ever asked me that before," Gabe answered as she took another sip of wine.

I put my glass on the countertop and moved even closer to her. I was staring directly into her onyx eyes, hypnotized by them. I felt as if I was looking directly into her soul.

"Well, I love women. I love everything about them, from the way they smell to the way they feel. I especially love the way they taste," I whispered. I was so close now, I could smell the wine on her breath.

"Yes, I know you do," she said softly, holding my stare. Gabe didn't answer my question and she didn't back away. It was as if she dared me to make the next move and that shit turned me on.

"Do you realize how very beautiful you are right now?" I asked.

When she attempted to say thank you, I put one of my French manicured nails to her mouth, then covered it with mine. I gently kissed her soft, full lips and then, as if instinctively, she opened her mouth to receive my tongue. I closed my eyes and tried to remember to breathe. We kissed, letting our tongues dance in celebration of what was to come.

"You are breathtaking," I said softly while gently stroking her cheek.

"Toma mi respira lejos, tambien."

"What does that mean?" I asked and was a little turned on by the Spanish.

"It means that you take my breath away, too."

We kissed again deeply and I began to explore her body with my hands. I touched her firm breasts, rubbing my thumb against her already hard nipples through her silk blouse, and she closed her eyes and gasped with pleasure.

"I've never been loved by a woman before," Gabe said. "I hope you'll be patient with my inexperience."

"I'll be patient and gentle," I promised. "Just do what comes naturally and let your body respond to my touch."

She held me tightly around my waist and pulled me closer to her. We were breathing hard and fast as we started to undress each other. I was amazed at how quickly Gabe had removed my blouse and bra, setting my big titties free with what seemed like one smooth motion. She grabbed them and kissed them, one then the other, before kneeling down to pull off my skirt, leaving me standing there wearing only a smile.

"Eres mas hermosa que una manana en el verano."

"What?" I asked.

"You are more beautiful than a summer morning," Gabe replied.

I could tell that she worked out because her body

was tight. Her breasts stood like two party hats and her ass was so tight, I could have bounced a quarter off of it. Her skin was as soft as a yellow rose. It was like butta, baby! I reached between her legs and she was dripping like a faucet, waiting to be turned on full force.

I wanted to move this party to my bedroom. Without a word, I took Gabe's hand and led her upstairs. She willingly followed.

I lit a few candles and we got into my bed. We held each other for awhile, stroking and caressing; becoming more familiar. I couldn't wait to taste her body. I started kissing her breasts, almost swallowing them whole. I suckled her hard nipples like an infant and then encircled them with my tongue like a lover. She let out a moan that came from deep within.

"That's it, baby. Let me make you feel good," I instructed.

I wanted to feel how soft she was inside. My tongue played with her swollen clit while I teased her hot opening with my fingertip. When I sensed she was on the verge of a total meltdown, I slowly slid them inside of her wetness and began to move them in and out, making her dance to my music. My tongue took a shine to her soft folds. She rode my hand and face until she came like a freight train and made almost as much noise. Her pussy muscles gripped my fingers and milked them for more. I licked my fingers, tasting her sweet sap. She tasted wonderful!

It seemed as if Gabe couldn't wait to return my not-so-random act of kindness. She started kissing me, letting her tongue explore every inch of my mouth. She moved down to my neck, licking and sucking until she found my spot and lingered there for what seemed like an eternity. She continued her trip down my entire body, like a tourist looking for her favorite attraction. Gabe made sure to give my nipples extra special attention with her tongue. They were like two chocolate-dipped nuts between her lips.

She finally made it to my ultimate pleasure point and I gladly opened my legs as wide as the Atlantic to give her full access to my rainforest. For a first timer, she was working it! I writhed and moaned as she worked her voodoo on my clit with her tongue and had me totally under her spell. I sat up a little; I had to watch this artist at work. Her eyes were closed and she was totally oblivious to anything other than my pleasure. I couldn't remember ever having someone this into me and it made my juices flow. I ran my fingers through her dark tresses, which covered my stomach as she greedily ate me.

I felt as if my entire body was on fire and more gasoline was being poured on. I grabbed her head and pushed it deeper into my damp muff as I came harder than ever and screamed her name. Gabe kissed her way up just as she had kissed her way down, which made me tremble with aftershock. She ran her hot tongue over my lips, letting me taste myself. We fell asleep together, totally satisfied.

The sun rose on our lovemaking the next morning. I introduced Gabe to Venus, my double dildo. After a quick crash course on how to use it, we glided ourselves onto it and went for a fabulous ride. We lay face to face and gyrated on its hardness, breathing each other's breaths and watching waves of ecstasy in each other's eyes. We held on to each other for dear life as we were both taken somewhere over the rainbow by earth-shattering orgasms that seemed to go on for days. We've been inseparable ever since that night.

Like all little girls, I dreamed of finding true love and living happily ever after in a big house, with a proverbial white picket fence. I have all of that and then some in Gabriella. As I drive down the interstate, with her asleep on the passenger's side and Pascal asleep in the backseat, I realize that fairy tales do indeed come true.

CONVENTION

CHERI CRYSTAL

I WAS WRITING "I so want to please you and tease you, lick you and fuck you" when the captain announced our final descent onto the runway at JFK International Airport. My stomach lurched and my ears clogged as the plane lost altitude. Looking out as we passed over the Belt Parkway, noticing the walkers and joggers on the promenade along the ocean, I sighed contentedly; it was wonderful to be back in the greatest city in the world.

I was born and raised in Brooklyn, but relocated for a lucrative position as an outpatient clinical psychotherapist at a women's mood disorder clinic in Baltimore. I missed the city and looked forward to staying at the midtown Manhattan hotel that was hosting the convention.

The hot balmy air hit me hard as I left the air-conditioned building and walked toward the shuttle waiting to transport me to the hotel. My thoughts and longing to see a particular woman made travel between the boroughs seem quicker. I replayed every scenario of our meeting in my mind as the traffic rolled by.

The hotel was nicer than I had imagined. From the outside, it looked like your typical skyscraper, but once inside, the lobby, decorated in early eighteenth-century English style furniture, was impressive. Queen Anne chairs upholstered in bizarre patterns of exotic flowers, birds, and animals, sat on either side of the marble fireplace. A large Buckingham settee with lacquered mahogany end tables faced the front desk. It gave the place a majestic feel. But the most memorable part of the hotel was the tall live sentry palms that reached toward vaulted ceilings. The hotel had a breathtaking atrium. As I wheeled my luggage past exquisite shops and restaurants, I felt as though I had entered a different world.

For the first time in years, I was single. I was my own person, with my own plans for how I was going to spend my time. Except I wouldn't be alone. Hundreds of women in all shapes and sizes attended this conference, but only one piqued my interest. My heart beat faster at the mere thought of her.

I met Susan at the last convention and we became fast friends. I thought she was extremely cute then, but I had a boyfriend. I vividly remember our conversation.

"I think, I have these feelings for, er, I want you," I said, over drinks.

"You're straight. I don't do straight, bi-curious women," she said delicately as if she was trying hard to spare my feelings.

"I know, I understand, but," I stammered, trying hard to express my feelings as coherently as possible and failing miserably.

"Look, you're beautiful, smart, sexy, and desirable, but I've learned the hard way that messing around with straight women is bad news." She was adamant about that but at the same time I detected a hint of regret in her voice.

"You're right," I agreed, but I felt the opposite. She was the first woman I ever really fell head over heels in lust with and I hadn't a clue what to do with these feelings. So much for being a psychotherapist! I was great at counseling others, but when it came to my own heart, I was lost.

Nothing happened, even though my physical and psychological attraction went beyond words, beyond comprehension. My mind and body were out of control and I wanted to touch her, tease her, and fuck her, but there wasn't a damn thing I could do about it. It was excruciating! When she rejected my advances I felt like I was punched in the stomach, but I didn't want to risk losing her friendship and so I vowed never to bring it up again. We kept in touch through e-mails and phone calls, planning to hang out again at the next convention. I couldn't wait. In our correspondence, I did my best to keep my feelings to myself—barely. Thoughts of her consumed my every waking moment and she even invaded my dreams.

Definitely not wanting to waste any time unpacking, I put my bags in my room, checked my look in the mirror, and ran down the stairs. I couldn't even wait for the elevator. I didn't realize then that I was going to become very familiar with the stairwell and look back on it fondly.

Vigilant and anxiously awaiting Susan's arrival, I wondered why she was late. When she hadn't arrived, I joined a few colleagues at a nearby restaurant to pass the time. Afterward, I went back to my room, stripped, and got into bed. Not even fifteen minutes elapsed before a loud jangling sound woke me. Almost asleep, I jumped up and couldn't figure out what that noise was. I turned on the light and realized it was the phone.

"Hello?" I said. I felt disoriented and a bit dizzy.

"I'm in the lobby. Want to join me for drinks?" she asked.

"I'm naked here," I replied, smiling as I recognized her voice.

"I'll be right up," she laughed.

Laughing too, I said, "What happened? I thought you were landing hours ago."

"Delays, missing my connecting flight in Atlanta, don't ask. Be up in a sec."

"Good." I dropped the phone back on the cradle.

As I threw on the crumpled clothes I had left on the floor I heard her knock. As much as I wanted to greet her wearing nothing but a smile, I couldn't do it. Nerves got the better of me as I tried to talk myself into behaving. *Calm down, girl. You don't want to scare the crap out of her and risk further rejection. She can't look as great as you remembered. No way.*

I opened the door.

Holy shit. She was a knockout. I couldn't breathe, I couldn't speak, I . . .

"Hey gorgeous!" she said and grabbed me for a hug.

Oh, I hugged her back all right. I hung on for dear life and never wanted to release her. The intoxicating scent of her hair filled me with insurmountable desire. She finally let me go and held me at arms length.

"Let me look at you," she said.

Gathering my strength and sucking in my breath, I gazed up into her deep blue eyes. Her thick lashes matched her thick, wavy jet-black hair. The short cut she wore emphasized her fire engine-red highlights. She had a wonderful way with strawberry and cream-scented mousse. A smattering of freckles lay across her nose and cheeks. Her full lips were more inviting than I remembered. My mouth was suddenly very dry, and I licked my lips to no avail.

She dropped the light jacket she had in the crook of her arm before we embraced. Brushing up against her white ribbed tank top, feeling her firm breasts pressed up against mine, made my nipples harden through my

T-shirt. She wasn't wearing a bra either.

"You are so fucking cute!" she said.

"So are you," I replied and changed the subject. I was getting too hot and horny for my own good, thinking I didn't want to leave the room. Ever.

"Should we go then?"

"Sure. Let's find a bar anywhere but downstairs. It's swarming with shrinks."

"Great," I said and took my room key. "Do I need my purse or should I just put my ID and some money in my pocket?"

"Nah, my treat." I started to protest but she put her hand over my mouth. I nearly bit her fingers, longing to devour them.

We left the hotel and chatted and laughed while searching for an inviting neighborhood bar. There were many choices. Despite the late hour, the streets and sidewalks were crowded with cabs and pedestrians doing the street-crossing dance, competing for the right-of-way. I wasn't surprised when people didn't pay attention to the traffic lights since New Yorkers always seem to be in a big fat hurry. That night I was in no rush to be anywhere else in the world. Everything was vibrant and alive with the nighttime hustle and bustle, which further confirmed that Manhattan is the city that never sleeps. I was acutely aware of lovers walking hand in hand and thought about Sue and me. Is that what I wanted for us?

It was a lovely night for a stroll with pleasant temperatures, great company, and bright lights adding a nice glow. We ended up in a semicrowded bar with a live jazz musician and stayed out longer than we should have. After I lost count of how many beers we'd consumed, we went back to the hotel. She walked me to my room.

"Well, I guess I'll see you in the morning at the first lecture, then," I said, trying to be strong, but wanting to ask her to stay with me instead. I didn't know how much longer I would last before I melted.

"Yep, I figure it will be a good place to catch up on our sleep." She laughed and I joined her. The more she lingered, the harder it was for me to keep my hands off her. Reluctantly, we gave each other a brief hug and said goodnight. It didn't take me long to please myself with a couple of quick strokes before I fell into a deep sleep.

The next day's schedule was chock full of lectures rehashing psychological modalities, clinical trials, studies, and findings, but even with the lack of sleep, I was bright-eyed and bushy-tailed. Infatuation and longing fueled my energy levels.

I spotted her during the continental breakfast at the sign-in table. She held a mug of coffee in one hand and a chocolate croissant in the other. She was much more delicious looking than the pastry, and I walked right up to her.

"Morning. Sleep well?" I asked, unable to stop myself from staring, mesmerized by the way her tongue licked the chocolate off her lips before she took a swig of steaming coffee. I longed to take a bite.

"Yeah, you?"

I nodded just as the doors opened, signaling that the first workshop was about to begin. We found seats and settled in for a long morning.

I kept my legs tightly crossed, and my body tingled every time she leaned into me to whisper some witty remark in my ear. Sue was hysterical and her keen sense of humor tickled more than just my funny bone. The lecturer outlined all the side effects of the various medications on the market for treating mood disorders, including eating disorders. Everyone knew the sexual side effects of the SSRIs, but just the mention of the word sex, and our ears perked up.

"Remind me never to take Prozac, Zoloft, or Paxil," she deadpanned.

"Me too," I agreed, and stifled a chuckle.

At the lunch break, I bolted from the room, needing air. My lustful thoughts ran away with me. I had to do something. Quickly. I raced past the vendor display tables and found the stairwell behind one of the booths. It was empty and not air conditioned like the chilly lecture halls. The warmth felt good. It wasn't until I felt her breath on my neck that I realized I wasn't alone.

I turned around and my nose bumped into her forehead. She stood two steps below me; we were face to face. I grabbed her head and pulled her lips toward mine. She parted my eager lips hungrily. I was reeling and just when I thought I would fall down the stairs, she scooped me up. With incredibly strong arms, she carried me to the landing. My kisses became more urgent and she followed my lead. I think I swallowed her Big Red gum and we both laughed.

Only when we stopped briefly for a breath did she try to speak. "You sure?" she asked, her gaze searching my face for an answer.

I never knew I could be this infatuated and sexually aroused by a woman. I couldn't imagine spending the rest of my life wondering, what if I had let her kiss me, what if I had let her make love to me.

"Yes, I want you so bad."

"What about your boyfriend?"

"We broke up."

She pulled me in tighter. The stairwell grew steamier by the second. She reached under my shirt and teased my taut nipples with her fingers. I moaned and threw back my head. She bit my neck and I nearly screamed with delight. I grabbed her earlobe between my teeth. Hungering for her, I nibbled at her neck and she caressed me with her hands.

"I want you too, so bad." She kissed me once more and put her hands around my butt, lifting me off the floor, hugging me to her. She put me down and I reached for her breasts. I had to touch her. I longed to make her scream.

"My room," I panted, and led her up another two flights before hand in hand we breathlessly entered the hall. Pulling her along with one hand, I managed to get out my key.

"No, let's go to my room," she said.

"But, why?"

"You'll see. Come on."

Once in her room it felt like the walls were spinning. Or, was it my head that was reeling? The unmade bed was a welcome sight. She had an inside room overlooking the atrium. The drapes were open so I could see the reception area filled with attendees lining up for lunch. We had about an hour and a half before the next workshop.

What was I thinking? Could my dream be coming true? Did I really want to do this? I never wanted to do something so badly and knew that if I did then things would never be the same. I would never be the same.

My thoughts were long forgotten as she began undressing me for real and not just with her eyes. There was something sensual about the way she looked at me with longing, completely mirroring my own desires.

I had to have this woman, I had to fuck her, and I had to have her fuck me. Simple. My shirt was the first thing to go. She quickly flung my bra onto the chair as well, taking my breasts in her hands and then in her mouth.

"You're so beautiful. You make me so hard," she said.

Being wanted and lusted after made me feel complete. I was soaring above the clouds with the wind in my hair.

"I've wanted you since we met," I said.

"Me too," Sue whispered, and continued to sweep me off my feet.

I could only kiss her as she then unzipped my slacks, and let them fall. My laced shoes made it impossible for me to kick them off but I was too busy to care. Hopping awkwardly, I moved in to take the bottom of her crew neck shirt out of her khakis and pull it over her head. I did the same with her sports bra and gazed at her rock hard nipples atop large, luscious, creamy white breasts. She was delicious. My stomach growled just then.

"You hungry?" she asked.

"For you," I purred. "Only for you."

She led me to the bed and gently pushed me down. Once I was on my back with my pants around my ankles and my legs dangling off the bed, she lifted my calves and pulled off my shoes. She then took off my panties and cast them aside before opening up my thighs. Her fingers parted my folds and she gently ran her thumb along the shaft of my clit. I grabbed tightly at her wrists when she moved her hands away.

"Touch me, *please*," I begged. "Don't ever stop."

"I never want to stop," she barely whispered. I could see the lust in her eyes, the sweat forming on her brow, and the way she moistened her lips with her tongue. I watched as she removed her pants and Jockeys, taking her boots off with them in one effortless swoop. When we were both completely naked, she grabbed me under my armpits and moved me up higher on the bed so she could straddle me with her knees. I had a great view of her big clit. I swallowed hard.

"Are you sure you want to do this? You said you broke up with Joe. But, are you sure it's a woman you want? I don't want you to have any regrets."

Tears welled up in my eyes and threatened to spill over onto the sheets. It was so sweet of her to worry about me. She was my friend first and now my lover. It was too good to be true.

"I don't want just any woman. I want you, Susan. Just you," I cried, as tears of joy streaked my cheeks. All of my pent-up emotions came pouring out. Knowing what I really wanted filled me with such relief. I finally knew who I was! Better late than never.

"Aw, I can't have you cry," she said.

"I'm not crying," I denied and wiped my tears with her help. "I want you more than you can imagine. I can't think of anything right now but you. Please fuck me," I said, and managed to smile.

She tenderly kissed away my tears and then she kissed my lips; I ferociously pulled her toward me. Tears forgotten, I picked up where we left off. Naked, our bodies melding together as one, breast-to-breast, torso-to-torso. It felt so right; I dove in with eyes wide open.

The more she sucked on my tits the wetter I became. By the time she took my pussy in her mouth she had to lap up my juices with her tongue. My hands tangled in her hair, and then I was digging into her back with my long, painted fingernails. She sucked, licked, and fucked me with her tongue until my body shook with the quickest, strongest orgasm I had had in years.

"Oh . . . God . . . that was fucking amazing." I kissed her hard on her lips. The smile she gave me was a gift, as if her talented tongue wasn't enough.

"Be right back," she said and got off the bed. I couldn't imagine where she was going and thought that maybe she had to pee.

When she strolled out of the bathroom with a strap-on, I felt my clit fill with desire once more. She looked so hot with her big fat cock nestled right below her trimmed black pubes. I opened my arms and legs, beseeching her to come over to me. She wasted no time after slipping a condom and lube all over her thick dick. I tugged at it, making sure I rubbed her clit as I did. She bit her lip and her eyes turned an even darker shade of blue. Mesmerized, I took her cock and placed it at the opening of my cunt.

"I am gonna fuck you so hard and good. I want your first time with a woman to be the best," she said, teasing me with her dick.

"It already is," I murmured, but was soon lost in the sweet sensation of her rocking in and out of me.

"Harder," I cried.

A few more thrusts and she shuddered. "God, I'm coming . . . you're . . . so . . . hot."

Watching her face as she came sent waves of another orgasm shaking me to the core. She flopped down beside me and I nestled my head into the crook of her arm with my leg folded and laying over her crotch just below her cock. It was a perfect fit—the two of us lying there with her arm under my neck. I kissed her cheek.

"Thank you," I said.

"*I* thank you, sweets."

"Mind if I try that thing on?" I said, indicating the cock. "I always wanted to see what it was like to be on top."

"Oh yeah?" She got up, took the contraption off, and helped me get it on. When it was all set, I laughed out loud.

"Damn, this feels so good. Who knew?" I felt a mischievous grin on my face as I came toward her.

"Oh no, you don't." She was backing away. "I see that look in your eyes."

"Why not? Don't you want me to fuck you this time? Don't you want me to make you come till you scream?" I teased.

I could see her resolve to get all butch on me and refuse to let me play. I backed her up into a corner of the room.

"Oh, no. No fucking way!"

But I ignored her, pressing my cock up against her wet pussy as I kissed every inch of her I could get my lips on. It wasn't long before I was able to persuade her onto the bed, on her back, with her legs spread wide. She had the most beautiful pussy I had ever seen, not that I had seen any up close and personal like this, but

I had seen pictures and trust me, she was gorgeous. I fumbled with the cock, trying desperately to control *it*, rather than the other way around, but I was not very successful.

"Wait, if you're going to do this, might as well do it right." She grabbed a fresh condom and some lube and greased me up before guiding the dick into her wet, waiting opening.

At first, the dildo kept slipping out and we ended up laughing so hard I couldn't breathe. After several attempts, I started to get the hang of it and gingerly thrust the cock in and out, but only going deeper when I was sure she was all right. Soon my rhythm picked up pace, I lost all track of time, and I fucked her until she came.

Forget about hell—I was in heaven. Afterward I let her just hold me, safe and warm. And maybe even loved but it was too soon to tell. I just knew that I never wanted that moment to end.

Not to spoil the mood but not wanting to get too serious just yet, I called, "Last one in the shower is a rotten egg."

She ran past me so fast I had to laugh as I joined her in the bathroom. "What about the next workshop? You said you needed the credits and wanted to learn a few things," she said. "Isn't that what a convention is for?" she teased.

"I think I've learned enough for one day." I kissed her full on the lips, lingering as I did it to emphasize my point. "And you are the most amazing and sexy teacher."

"You're pretty sexy yourself." She caught my lower lip in her teeth.

"We can go back after our shower," I suggested with a seductive smile.

"Maybe," she said and helped me soap up.

We never did make it to the afternoon sessions, but I discovered every inch of her luscious body as she learned exactly what it took to make me scream. We continue to look back fondly on the magic of Manhattan when lust took us by surprise and love was its reward.

HANDS FREE

RACHEL KRAMER BUSSEL

"MAKE LOVE TO me," Maria said, her lips curved into what can only be called a catlike grin, "but don't use you hands. Or your cock. In fact, don't even touch me at all. Make your love come inside me, give it to me the way I know you can," she continued, her eyes boring into mine. She was lying next to me in bed, so close and yet, apparently, so far. I didn't have a clue what she wanted me to do, but part of why I love her is because she goes off on tangents that seem to only make sense in her head—or at least, I don't get them.

Was she trying to send me on a wild goose chase, running around our small apartment picking up mementos, photos, trivia clues to show her what I could express best by sliding my fingers easily along her thigh, upward until I reached the spot that told me she loved me back? We'd always done our best communicating in bed, sheets tossed overboard like so much unnecessary baggage, bodies entwined, sweating, twisting, tearing, biting. I didn't need to look right at her when I could coil around her like a snake, my lips against her back while my torso wrapped around her hip, my hands everywhere at once.

But make love to her without touching her? At all? Somehow, I could tell from her voice that that didn't mean breaking out my favorite melts-in-your-pussy cyberskin dildo, the one that we both swore we'd leave the other for if only it could talk. Alas, even lying against the bed, her deeply tanned skin glowing against the crisp white sheets, thin arm flung under her, mani-cured red nails brushing against the headboard, she managed to convey not the carefree woman I knew and loved, but someone demanding something next to impossible.

But I'm always up for a challenge, and maybe Maria knew something I didn't.

"Okay, I'll show you, or rather, tell you, but I want you to wear the blindfold. I'm going to whisper in your ear but it's too much if you're looking at me as well." Strange how we can be so intimate, day after day, year after year, yet I could only bare my soul to her behind masked eyes. She nodded, and I reached into the drawer beneath our bed for the simple black eye mask, easily slipping it over her head. She sank back against the pillows, and I did, too, letting my mind go, and simply bearing my heart.

"Remember the time we were at Baskin-Robbins, and that little kid dropped his cone on the ground and was wailing? And you'd been telling me all day how much you wanted a cone of rocky road. I could see that greedy look on your face as the clerk handed you the cone, the way yours eyes lit up, the way you almost dropped yours too when he started to cry. And then, without a second thought, you just handed the kid yours, and he took a lick and then gave you the sloppiest, chocolaty smile on earth? I thought your cheeks would freeze the way you smiled back at him. That, Maria Sandoval, is when I knew I wanted to have your babies.

"But that wasn't when I knew I loved you. You know I don't believe in love at first sight, but I think when you went to bat against me in that class, and we pretty much monopolized all of Women's Studies 102 arguing about subjectivity and postmodernism, and you just had this spark about you. Plus, you simply wouldn't quit, and I was beginning to get the feeling that you just wanted the chance to spar—with me. That was the clincher, the way your face seemed to stay locked on Professor Taylor, but your eyes remained on me. When I saw the way they flared, I knew I had to have you for myself someday, even though I had you pegged for a mouthy straight girl who just didn't know when to be quiet. I was scared, though, and just couldn't see myself approaching you—you had to be the one to make the first move. But you're a lot more than meets the eye. You're a flirt who'll have anyone in any room eating out of the palm of your hand, but it takes quite a bit of work to get you into bed." I paused, remembering just how long it had taken, and how by the time we did finally entwine ourselves on her 300-thread-count sheets, I was already a goner. I'd thought of myself as stoic, stubborn, not letting anyone get under my skin, but without even seeming to try, my favorite femme had me wrapped around her manicured little finger.

She picked me up at the Mermaid Parade, while dressed as one of those seductive sirens, turquoise sarong and shell bikini, covered in glitter, wearing a long black fall, the fake hair tripping down her back. She did it all in giant platforms, so at first I thought she was taller. She came up to me and batted her insanely long fake eyelashes, then handed me a lollipop. "Suck it," she said, then smiled and walked away. I couldn't tell if that was all part of the festivities. I barely recognized her behind all the artifice, but my body got a familiar tingling feeling, and when she came up to me later, she teased me about it. "You don't recognize me, do you, Cat?" she asked, then slowly removed the fall, shaking out her own naturally dark, luxurious hair. When I finally figured out that she was my college crush, I gasped—no wonder I'd reacted so strongly! She stepped closer, and even though people were milling about all around us, it felt like just the two of us baking in the hot Coney Island sunshine. She leaned closer, so her lips brushed against mine when she said, "Ride the Cyclone with me."

Maybe I fell in love with her that very second, because I'd always sworn I would never ride the classic, and, in my opinion, rickety roller coaster, no matter how famous it was. I'd stood below it plenty of times and listened to the shrieks as passengers did that massive drop, some brave souls raising their hands in the air, coming off looking almost high from the adrenaline. But the very thought made me queasy. "I'll hold your hand," she sing-songed, pressing her sweaty, glittery body against mine. I didn't care if she ruined my white shirt or what she did to me as she pulled out all the stops to get me to go on what I'd dubbed the ride of death. "You'll be fine, Cat, I promise—I've ridden it dozens of times. Sixty-seven, to be precise. I'll make it worth your while," she said, and I wondered where this flirty seductress had been during our youthful college days.

I agreed, and as we stood on line, I almost had to pinch myself to make sure this was really happening, that I was really standing in line for the Cyclone with the woman who'd haunted my dreams—day and night—all four years of school. When we got in, the attendant snapped us into the little seat, our asses and legs touching. She simply dazzled, and not just because of the glitter. We started to ride upward as they boarded more passengers, and I gazed down at the crowd, the Boardwalk, the subway, the water. She looked right along with me, then said, "Beautiful, isn't it?" before grabbing my hand. She squeezed it, her fingers and palm warm, reassuring me that we'd be fine, and then she rested her head on my shoulder like she'd done it a thousand times, and I knew then she was a keeper. Her head felt so right, and she didn't seem to mind when I practically broke her fingers, crushing them in my grip when I found out the famed ride was just as perilous a freefall as it had always looked from the ground.

That was just the start of a budding friendship, one tinged with flirtation and kisses until we finally consummated our passion, and from then on, we spent all our free time together. I got so used to her, I felt weird being alone, and loved getting to know her quirks and habits, laughing at some, thrilling at others. When we'd go out to eat, she always ordered something sensuous, and even if she didn't, she'd somehow turn it into an erotic feast. The lady and the tramp had nothing on the way she twirled her spaghetti, always letting one last, lone piece of pasta get sucked into her mouth, so all I could do was look at those pretty pursed lips pulling the string of food inside them. She's tiny and curvy, but made sure to order dessert at every meal, and always gave me some, offering me a dollop of whipped cream with a scoop of her fingers.

But she wasn't just playing games. I continued to recite her virtues as she lay there, patiently listening. "You're a vixen, but you know when to put it all out there and when less equals more. You find ways to draw attention to yourself, with your push-up bras and always plunging necklines. But when I had to give that speech in front of our whole year, there you were in your little suit giving me a thumbs up and smiling discreetly." We both smiled at the memory, and I wondered when I'd get to kiss her, taste her, devour her. Her body always seems to be beckoning me forward, asking me questions I can only answer with my lips or hands, questions that I know I'll need a lifetime to properly reply to.

"You can be very stubborn, Maria Sandoval, and you know how to get what you want, but you also know what I need as well. When you were away visiting your family for a month, that could've broken us, or at least caused some cracks. But every day I came home to long, flowing letters, and then those flowers, for no other reason than you wanted me to smile. I did, and then I cried, because they were so lush, so vibrant, and I knew the florist hadn't been the one to pick them out. I love you because you are a born and bred New Yorker who embraces everything about this city, even the ice cream trucks screaming past our window. On those days when I'm ready to practically murder everyone on the subway train, when you're with me, you nuzzle up against me, tap your foot against mine, and smile all cool and calm and serene, like you're not being smashed next to all of humanity."

I looked down at her, tracing my pale fingers along her tanned skin, thinking of all the times she'd made me laugh and smile, how she'd shown me my very own city all over again. She has this way of taking over a sidewalk, of uncovering a hidden street, of grabbing me and pulling me deep into a park just to smell the flowers. She's the kind of girl who'll scour *Time Out New York* for every new gallery opening, obscure film, and unusual event. Last weekend, we did a scavenger hunt that took us to all five boroughs, and while I felt a little silly climbing a tree in Queens and barging into the W Hotel's bathroom in Manhattan, we had such a fabulous time. Some people say New York is too much—too much noise, too much excitement, too fast, too crowded—but Maria loves every second of it. "Mar, you just are this city, you're every facet of it, you're fast and wild and full of energy. You seem like you never sleep, even though when you do, it's snuggled up next to me looking so cute I just want to kiss you all over. You're one of those rare souls who really does want to see if she can make it through every restaurant in *Zagat*, and you make me want to explore right along with you. Sometimes it's a challenge to keep up with you, but you never make me feel lazy about it, and you delight in the simplest of pleasures, from street fairs to jungle gyms—remember that time you almost got stuck in the swing? You're lucky you're so tiny, and that you had me to rescue you.

"I love you because you make everything in my life brighter, better, more beautiful. I love getting your IM's during the day, love being able to meet you for lunch in Bryant Park, love that even as I glare at the last panhandler to get on my nerves or want to brush by the ever present tourists asking directions, you stop for each and every one of them. I love that you make me want to be a better person—not just for you, but for me too," I said, amazed that I'd let all that gush out of me so freely. I looked down at her striking black hair tussled all around her head, then lifted the blindfold to let her sleepy eyes drink me into their depths. I leaned down to give her a light peck on the cheek, and she pulled me closer, her tongue meeting mine.

"Cat, you're incredible. I knew you loved me, but I've never heard you say all those things." She took my hand and placed it over her heart, so I could hear it beating, steady and sure, pulsating against my fingers. "Now come here and make love to me for real," she said. And you can be sure I did exactly that.

ABOUT THE
CONTRIBUTORS

RACHEL KRAMER BUSSEL authors smut of all kinds. She also serves as senior editor at *Penthouse Variations*, writes the "Lusty Lady" column for *The Village Voice*, and hosts In the Flesh Erotic Reading Series. Her erotica anthologies include *Ultimate Undies, Sexiest Soles, Secret Slaves, Naughty Spanking Stories from A to Z 1 and 2, Up All Night, First-Timers, Glamour Girls: Femme/Femme Erotica,* and *Caught Looking: Erotic Tales of Voyeurs and Exhibitionists,* with more on the way. When she's not writing porn, she can be found blogging about cupcakes at cupcakestakethecake.blogspot.com. Find out more at www.rachelkramerbussel.com.

DIANA CAGE's books include *Box Lunch, Threeways, Bottoms Up,* and the forthcoming *Girl Meets Girl.* She's the managing editor of *Velvetpark* magazine and regularly writes about sex and relationships for a variety of publications. More of her work can be seen at www. dianacage.com.

W. S. CROSS is the author of the novel *Beyond You & Me,* the story of a woman's erotic journey of self-discovery at the dawn of the feminist movement. In addition to the novel, Cross's stories have appeared in *Clean Sheets* and *Tit-Elation.*

CHERI CRYSTAL is a health care professional by day and a writer of lesbian erotica and romance by night. She has stories in *Lessons in Love: Erotic Interludes 3,* edited by Radclyffe and Stacia Seaman; *After Midnight, True Lesbian Erotic Confessions,* edited by Chelsea James; and is currently working on a romance novel.

AMIE EVANS is a widely published creative nonfiction and literary erotica writer and author of the online-column "Two Girls Kissing." Evans is also an editor, experienced workshop provider, and a retired burlesque and high-femme drag performer. She is on the board of directors for Saints and Sinners LGBTQ literary festival and graduated Magna cum Laude from the University of Pittsburgh with a B.A. in Literature. She is currently working on her M.L.A. at Harvard.

LYNNE JAMNECK is a naughty girl who doesn't look it. She's also a complete geek, a *Battlestar Galactica* fan and a biter of hypocrites. Her dirty little secret is that she's a fool of a romantic at heart. Her short fiction has appeared in *Best Lesbian Erotica 2003/2006; Sex in The System: Stories of Erotic Futures, Technological Stimulation, and the Sensual Life of Machines; So Fey: Queer Faery Fictions*; and *Best Lesbian Romance 2007.* She blogs at www.lynne-jamneck.blogspot.com.

ILSA JULE lives in New York City where she spends some of her time writing. She wishes to thank Elizabeth Grainger for countless hours of editorial assistance and guidance.

GENEVA KING (www.genevaking.com) has been published in several anthologies including *Ultimate Lesbian Erotica 2006, Best Women's Erotica 2006, Ultimate Undies, Caramel Flava,* and *Travelrotica for Lesbians.* She intends to publish a book, if her professors ever give her enough time to do so.

MARILYN JAYE LEWIS is the award-winning author of *Neptune & Surf,* a trio of erotic novellas, called "a sensational debut" by the U.K.'s *Guardian* newspaper. Her short stories and novellas have been published worldwide and translated into French, Italian, and Japanese. Her popular erotic romance novels include *When Hearts Collide, In the Secret Hours,* and *When the Night Stood Still.* She is the founder of the Erotic Authors Association. Upcoming novels include *Freak Parade, A Killing on Mercy Road,* and *Twilight of the Immortal.*

HAZEL MILLS attended the University of Alabama and Springhill College majoring in business. She now resides with her family in Birmingham. She enjoys writing literary and erotic fiction. She is currently working on her first book, which will contain a collection of short erotic stories.

CHERYL MOCH, writer and playwright, was born and raised in Brooklyn, New York. She has lived in lower Manhattan for many years. Her play, *Cinderella: The Real True Story*, published by Metheun, has been produced in New York, London, and many other cities. It's also a happy love story, set in a place even more mythical than New York City.

KATIA NOYES's first novel, *Crashing America*, was a BookSense Notable Book and was chosen as one of the Ten Best Gay/Lesbian Books of 2005 by Amazon.com and the United Kingdom's Rainbow Network. It was also nominated for the Northern California Book Award, Publishing Triangle Award, and Lambda Literary Award. Her short stories have been published by Cleis and Down There Press. She lives in San Francisco.

RUTHANN ROBSON is the author of the lesbian novels *A/K/A* and *Cecile*, as well as numerous other works of lesbian fiction, creative nonfiction, poetry, and theory. She is professor of law at the City University of New York School of Law.

RACHEL ROSENBERG is twenty-three years old and lives in Montreal, Quebec. Some of the things that inspire her are: people-watching, fairytales, finding art on the street, girls with tangled hair, black coffee, people who carry notebooks with them, and natural sunlight. Aside from writing, she adores reading, watching indie films, and making collages.

KAREN TAYLOR used short stories to seduce author Laura Antoniou, and has been happily married to her since 1998. She has stories in *Friday the Rabbi Wore Lace, My Lover, My Friend, Best Transgender Erotica, First Person Sexual*, and is a contributing writer to *The Academy, Tales of the Marketplace*. Karen is the director of SAGE/Queens, an LGBT senior center in New York City.

YOLANDA WALLACE lives in historic Savannah, Georgia, with her partner of five years. A writer since childhood, she has recently taken up photography. She can often be found wandering around trying to capture on film the elusive image she sees in her head. She is currently at work on her latest (unpublished) novel.